HEART STOPPER

Heart Stopper

JILLIAN DODD

Editor: Jovana Shirley, Unforeseen Editing, www.unforeseenediting.com

Jillian Dodd Inc.
Seminole, FL

ISBN: 978-1-962549-37-0

BOOKS BY JILLIAN DODD

Eastbrooke Academy®
Best Friends Aren't Forever
Popularity Isn't Easy
Kisses Don't Stay Secret
First Loves Are Hard To Forget

London Prep®
The Exchange
The Boys' Club
The Kiss
The Key
The Party
The Country House
The Choice
The Club
The Match

The Keatyn Chronicles®
Stalk Me
Kiss Me
Date Me
Love Me
Adore Me
Hate Me
Get Me
Fame
Power
Money
Sex
Love
A Very Keatyn Christmas
Keatyn Unscripted
Aiden

That Boy®

That Boy
That Wedding
That Baby
That Love
That Ring
That Summer
That Promise
That Forever
That Crush
That Girl
That Someday

Dating in the City

Writing Mr. Right
Heart Stopper
Crazy For You
Catching Feelings
Party of One
Save the Date
Urban Cowboy
Check, Please!
Happily Ever Afters

Crawford Brothers

Vegas Love
Broken Love
Fake Love

Spy Girl®

The Prince
The Eagle
The Society
The Valiant
The Dauntless
The Phoenix
The Echelon

Girl off the Grid

WELL? ARE YOU gonna do it? Or are you gonna sit there and stare at it?"

I know I shouldn't since this is an important moment and my best friend is already annoyed with me for hemming and hawing and doing anything I can to avoid what needs to happen.

But I can't help it.

"That's what she said," I quip, chuckling at my own rather lame and outdated joke.

Hayley merely rolls her eyes. "I knew you were going to say that as soon as the words were out of my mouth."

And why not? We've known each other for years. She's the sister I never had.

Because she's known me for so long, she knows too well what's going on here. I can't hide much from her.

"You're stalling."

"Am not." Why don't I fold my arms and stick out my tongue while I'm at it? Maybe I can threaten to hold my breath until I get my way. That would be super mature.

"Are too." She taps the device sitting between us in the center of the table. "All you have to do is activate the spinner and let it tell you who you're gonna date next. It's pretty simple."

Pretty simple. Easy for her to say.

Ever since my editor informed me of my tanking book sales and basically dumped all over my writing style, life has been … interesting. It was Hayley who came up with the idea for this spinner thingy she created, where all I have to do is take a spin and let fate decide the trope I'll be tackling in my next book.

Only it's not so simple. I'll be seeking out and dating the type of man indicated by the spinning wheel. Because I love to torture myself.

"You know you need to get started on a new book."

At least she sounds mildly sympathetic and concerned. She isn't all but prostituting me, the way my editor would gladly do. Maggie even recommended I participate in a three-way, for Pete's sake. I mean, there's plenty I'm willing to do for my art and my career, but a girl's got to have limits.

"Yeah, I know that," I mutter in spite of her attempts at being kind. "I can hear the clock ticking in my head all the time. *Tick-tock, Kitty Valentine. Your career's going down the flusher if you don't spin up a new story—and fast*!" If we weren't in public, I'd fold my arms on top of the high-top table and bury my head in them.

Actually, that sounds pretty good. I think I'll do that.

"Get up," Hayley groans, shoving my shoulder just a little. "Now's not the time for drama. Now's the time for taking a chance, having a little fun. This is only the first step."

The thing is, it's not like I've never done this before. My latest book, cleverly titled *Her Billionaire Boss—really, couldn't Maggie have come up with something better than that?*—is based loosely upon the semi-relationship I had with my actual boss, Blake Marlin. The spinner led me to him—or at least to the boss trope.

It just so happens my boss is a billionaire. I killed two tropes with one stone—or something like that.

All joking aside, the time I spent with Blake was invaluable. No way would I have known how to describe the inside of a private jet or the sort of restaurants he took me to without having spent time with him. I would never have imagined flying halfway across the country just for dinner or making a phone call and coming up with the most incredible seats to a show that'd been sold out since the day tickets first went on sale.

I would also not have imagined how punishing that life could be for a man without a sense of work-life balance. Don't get me wrong. I don't have so much as a scrap of that balance myself. I'm the queen of working until all hours, foregoing sleep and personal hygiene in the face of a looming deadline.

But I'm not a media mogul either. I don't have assistants calling me at all hours of the day and night. I can go to a show or dinner without having it interrupted by some emergency or another.

What's the point of having all that money and freedom if it can't be enjoyed?

Which is a big part of what broke us up.

Now, I have to put myself through it again?

"You're not the one who's going through this," I have no choice but to remind Hayley. "You're not the one who has to meet these men and get to know them and maybe care for them a lot, only to leave them, so you can move on to the next one."

Rather than offering sympathy, she tosses her ridiculously glossy blonde hair over her shoulders and fixes me with a knowing look. "Listen, you know I love you."

"You sure sound like it right now."

"I do, and what I'm about to say comes from a place of love." She folds her hands on the table. "You're taking this too seriously."

That gets a laugh out of me, though there isn't exactly any humor in it. "Uh, okay. Thanks for that brilliant legal assessment."

"I'll let that one slide since you're feeling some type of way. This doesn't have to be as fraught with emotion as you're making it out to be. Okay, so you fell a little too hard for Blake. Lesson learned. You can't let yourself get all mixed up in your feelings this time around."

"Easier said than done."

"Maybe you'll get lucky, and this next guy will be a real jerk you couldn't possibly fall in love with." She shrugs before signaling for another round of drinks.

It's happy hour, meaning the bar is packed with young business types just getting off work for the day. Considering how desperate they all seem for a drink, I'm glad I don't work in a stressful office.

Though my work can be stressful enough. There's a reason so many infamous writers also happened to be alcoholics.

"I don't want to end up hurting again, is all. You know how much I liked Blake. It's only been a month since we broke things off."

"You didn't even sleep with him."

"So? What's that got to do with anything?"

"I'm just saying, I could see catching feelings if you had gone all the way."

"Gone all the way? What is this? A teen movie from the eighties?" I snort.

"*Fucked*, okay? You didn't fuck him."

Needless to say, several pairs of eyes turn our way.

"Not that he didn't want to," I explain to these random strangers. "Because he did. He super did. We were totally gonna … bone."

"Oh my God," Hayley groans, picking up her fresh martini and downing half of it in one gulp.

"Anyway, I don't see what that has to do with it," I whisper once everybody goes back to minding their own darn business. "You can have feelings for somebody without doing it."

"I'm only trying to give you a little perspective, okay? That's all. You take life too seriously."

"Says the lawyer."

"Stop wasting time. Spin the damn thing and get this over with. You're killing me with all this procrastination."

Call me childish, but the fact that she's so dead set on me doing it makes me even more determined to dig my heels in and refuse. Only she has a point—okay, many good points—and the thought that Maggie will straight-up murder me if I don't start producing more work gets me to spin.

"Finally," Hayley sighs. "What's it gonna be? Sexy firefighter? Sexy single daddy? Sexy Santa?"

"Will you lay off the Santa idea?" I laugh. "Besides, it's not the right time of year for that."

"What can I say? I have a thing for sitting on guys' laps." She says it just loudly enough to attract attention from a twenty-something with a killer smile and a custom suit, who's been hovering nearby throughout our conversation. "Don't get any ideas," she warns him when he sidles up next to her, which is enough to shoo him away.

"You're too good at that," I marvel.

She's had practice. The girl attracts men like bees to honey.

"Ooh! Doctor!" she gasps, clapping ecstatically. "How exciting!"

"A doctor? How am I supposed to find a doctor to date?" I ask in despair. "What, do I fake an injury and go to the ER?"

"You could do worse." She shrugs. "And knowing you and your clumsiness, it probably won't take long for a real injury to send you there."

"Sometimes, I wonder if you even like me," I sigh.

"I do. I love you." Even though she kicks me under the table when she says it, I believe her. She didn't kick all that hard. It was more of a loving nudge. "I'm only trying to add a little levity. As for how to find one ..."

She taps her chin, looking up at the ceiling while I start in on the drink, which has been sitting untouched all this time. After drinking way too much and throwing up in my hot neighbor's apartment, I've been playing it cool with the booze. Not that I'm a big drinker, which is probably why it didn't take all that much to get me to that awful state.

"Duh!" She smacks the table with both hands. "A dating profile. You can set one up and look for doctors in the city who are single and interested in dating."

Here's the thing: I'm a writer. A darn good one. Four number-one best sellers can't be wrong.

But that's not the same as writing about myself.

"I've never written one of those before," I admit, playing with my glass. "I mean, how do I make myself look datable?"

"Uh, put a picture of yourself on the Internet and say, *I'm available*, babe." She grins. "They'll come running."

"Will not," I scoff.

"Yeah, they will. And if your gorgeous face doesn't do it, there's always the fact that you're a successful author. A career woman with her act together."

"Great. Now, I have to get my act together too?" I groan.

"No," she assures me, shaking her head. "Just pretend to. All you have to do is attract a likely candidate and get him on the hook, and then you're golden."

"You could have at least humored me and said I already had my act together." I pout.

She reaches across the table, taking my hand. "Honey," she murmurs, looking me straight in the eye, "we both know you don't."

"I can always count on you." I smile.

Chapter Two

"FOR A WRITER, you're not very good at this." Hayley leans over my shoulder to peer at the screen, where the results of endless typing and deleting and typing again … and deleting again await her scrutiny.

"Like I said, I can't write about myself. It's hopeless. I come off sounding like a corny Goody Two–shoes," I mutter.

"I'm sure it's not that bu—oh. You do." She winces.

"See?"

"Why don't you let me write it for you?" she suggests. "It's always easier for friends to point out all the good qualities in a person. We don't see those things in ourselves, you know? Even if we do, we can't describe them."

"Hmm … I don't know." I look her up and down, arching an eyebrow. "Can I trust you?"

"For Pete's sake, you can delete it if you don't like it," she groans, nudging me out of my chair. "Move it, girlie. We don't have the rest of our lives to get this done. You have a book to write."

Yes, and she has work she's putting aside to help me with this. The life of an attorney at a high-profile firm is crazy busy, and the fact that she's even taking the time to hang out with me is a big deal.

"Fine, fine." My stomach lurches, but I get out of the way and let her take a seat.

"Okay, let's get rid of all this mumbo jumbo," she says, deleting everything I labored over for the last twenty minutes.

"But I thought the part about looking for a happy ending was cute."

That earns me an eye roll. "You're not five years old. You're a hot, single career woman who's in the mood for a doctor's skillful touch."

"Tell me you're not going to put that in there," I beg while walking to the kitchen for some much-needed sustenance.

We never got to the food part of our little date since Hayley was so gung ho about getting back to my apartment, so we could work on my profile together.

Really, she's the best friend I could ever ask for.

"No, you dork," she calls out. Maybe I was wrong about the best-friend thing. "We can't make it look obvious that you're in the market for a doctor. That'll look too desperate and scare them off."

"Good point. This is why I keep you around." There are cheese, pears, and grapes in the fridge, crackers in the pantry. I put together a little plate for us and take it out to her.

"And this is why I keep you around." She pops a chunk of Humboldt Fog into her mouth while pointing to the screen.

"Successful romance author looking for a little real-life sizzle," I murmur as I read. "Okay, I can live with that." I mean, it's not perfect, but it'll do. I wasn't faring much better. Who am I to judge?

"I thought we should keep the romance writer part in there," she confides with a wink, fingers flying over the keys even though she's looking up at me. It's unnerving, how she can talk to me while thinking about whatever it is she's typing.

"How come?"

"People assume a romance writer will be good in bed." When I throw a scowl her way, she shrugs. "I don't make the rules. That's what people think."

"Who are these people? Where are you getting this from?"

"A few people I know. What?" she asks, laughing when I pull another skeptical face. "I brag about you from time to time. You're my best friend, and I'm proud. And sometimes, I'll get the wiggly eyebrows." She demonstrates, brows lifting up and down.

"What? Do they think I'm practicing my sexy moves on you or something?"

"Who knows? People have dirty minds. Anyway"—she crooks a finger, and I lean in again—

"just about anyone familiar with romance knows the name Kitty Valentine," she assures.

I cut her a look from the corner of my eye. "You might be exaggerating a little bit."

"Oh, gee, I didn't know you'd have to submit W-2s and references," she whispers, nudging me back toward the screen.

With a sigh, I continue, "*But that's the thing about being a* New York Times *bestseller—all that writing leaves little time for dating. This is where you might come in.*"

"Too braggy?" she asks before reaching for more cheese and fruit.

"Eh." I stand back, arms folded. "Is anybody who visits the site going to be able to read this?"

"No, they don't have to. You can mark your profile as Private, and only people you've reached out to will be able to see it."

"That's nice to know." I read her opening lines again. "Okay. Good start. I can live with that."

"Oh, thank you, Great One." She laughs before turning back to the keyboard. "I'll take that as high praise, coming from you."

"You should."

We both jump at the knock on my front door.

"Expecting someone?" Hayley asks.

"Does it look like I am?" I'm frozen in place. People don't randomly knock on my front door. Funny, but in a city filled with millions of others, the idea of someone dropping by is completely foreign. I have to fight the impulse to pretend I'm not home.

Another knock.

"Well?" Hayley whispers. "Are you going to let them stand there forever?"

I'm about to say yes, that's exactly what I want to do, when a voice rings out. "Hello? There's a lady's wallet lying in the hallway, and the ID says it belongs to somebody named Kathryn. I don't know of any Kathryn living here ..."

"Jeez," I mutter, jogging for the door in my bare feet. It's only Matt.

Matt is leaning against the doorframe, smirking his most Matt-like smirk, holding up my wallet for inspection. "You don't pay much attention to pesky things like where your wallet ends up, do you?"

"To think, I was about to thank you for picking this up for me," I groan, reaching for it.

"Not so fast." He pulls it just out of my grasp. "What were you doing, leaving your wallet out here so I'd think you were kidnapped or something?"

"I wasn't exactly thinking about you when I dropped it, Matt. This might come as a surprise, but you don't play a part in my every thought. Sorry about that." I reach for it again, but he's too stinking tall. And I'm at a disadvantage with my heels lying on the floor behind me.

"Who is this?" Hayley shows up behind me, an arm on my shoulders.

Stupid, predictable Matt. His hazel eyes travel

over her, first head to toe and then back up again while he strokes the brown scruff covering his chin. It's like this all the time, whenever a new man meets my painfully gorgeous best friend.

Only I happen to know what a horndog he is and how successful he is with the ladies.

Crap. Am I going to have to live through listening to Hayley getting pounded just on the other side of my office wall? Because I've heard enough female orgasms to last me the rest of my life—fake or real, they were loud as heck—and I could live without hearing hers.

Especially if it's Matt who happens to be giving it to her.

Though that shouldn't matter, should it? No way. He's just … Matt. The guy who lives across the hall.

"Hayley Craig." She thrusts her hand toward him. "Best friend."

"Matt Ryder." He grins before shaking her hand. "Neighbor and occasional beer buddy."

"Oh?" Her wide, questioning eyes turn my way.

"Don't look at me." I shrug. "I didn't know I had to clear new people by you."

"You should know by now. I can't have you making random friends. That means I can't run their name through every database at my firm's disposal." She turns back to Matt, still smiling.

"That's R-Y-D-E-R."

Honestly, I think Hayley's met her match. He's

not the slightest bit ruffled. Most men with common sense would back away, hands raised, and disappear behind their door. And lock it. And put the chain in place.

"I'll make a note of that." She looks at me and then at him again. "What are you up to? We were putting together a—"

"No, no, no," I call out over her. "Nope. No way. It's a girls' night."

"You want your wallet back?" Matt holds it up again. "Tell me what you're doing that you don't want me to know. If it's something weird and female, I don't need to be a part of it."

"Weird and female?" I snort. "What? Do you think we're testing tampons to see which brand we like best?"

"Or maybe we're performing some weird, witchy ritual to punish our ex-boyfriends," Hayley suggests. "It's been a while since I summoned a demon, and I think it's a full moon."

Rather than leave it there, she blurts out, "Dating profile. We're making a dating profile for her." By the time she finishes, I'm swatting at her like I'd swat at any pest. "I'm sorry!" She ducks away from me, giggling, and runs back to the laptop.

"Dang it!" I growl as my heart sinks.

Matt's smiling from ear to ear in that insufferable way of his. Of course.

"A dating profile? What, the whole dating-for-a-book thing isn't working? This is big news."

"It isn't. And it's in service of the dating-for-a-book thing, which, by the way, I don't appreciate being called a thing. And what are you doing?" I demand when he slides past me to get into the apartment. I mean, okay, I could've tried a little harder to stop him, but he's bigger than me, and he's holding my wallet.

"You can't tell me you're making up a profile and not expect me to be interested in it." He's too quick and is already reading over Hayley's shoulder before I can stop him.

"Come on. This is ridiculous. Give me the wallet, please."

He hands it over without looking, too busy reading. "So, you're trying to pick up your next boyfriend this way?" he asks, a grin spreading his generous mouth.

I used to want to kiss that mouth—I mean, I have eyes and I'm a girl who likes men and he's definitely a man and whatnot—but now?

Now, I sorta want to smack him a little.

"You know how this goes. I'm looking for a very specific type of person."

"What type?" He quirks an eyebrow, folding his arms.

He can't wait to hear this, I can tell. Which, of course, makes me want to hold my breath until I pass out because I'd rather do that than hear him laugh at me.

Hayley, as always, can be relied upon. "A doctor."

"Thanks," I mutter as Matt starts laughing especially hard.

"What's so wrong with me dating a doctor?" I demand.

Darned if he doesn't have to wipe tears from his eyes. "Sorry. That struck me as funny."

"No kidding. Answer my question."

"There's nothing wrong with it." He shrugs. "It's more the idea of having to go on a dating site to find the next poor sucker."

There's something about having known someone for so long and as well as Hayley and I know each other. You start to share part of your brain—which is why it's convenient Hayley's practically a certifiable genius. She has brain to spare.

"Poor sucker?" we both shout loud enough and perfectly in sync enough that we practically knock him backward onto the sofa. As it is, he nudges it a little with the backs of his legs, and his jaw is practically on the floor.

"I give! I give! I should know better than to try to handle two women at once!"

"Do my poor ears and imagination a favor and keep that in mind when you're trying to pick up your next girl for the night, okay?"

His eyes twinkle in an instant before he smirks. "I never have a problem with that."

Hayley looks him up and down. "I think I like you."

"Oh?"

Her brow lowers. "Not that way."

"Oh." He shrugs at me. "You gotta try, right?"

"No, you don't gotta try." I twirl one finger in the air. "About-face, please, and let us get back to work. This is important. You don't see me coming around and … I don't know, making fun of the reports you ran this morning."

"Please," Hayley begs. "It took me long enough to get her to agree to do this in the first place. Don't distract her now."

"Since you put it that way, I'll see myself out." He whistles softly as he walks to the door. "If you need any inspiration for a particularly filthy scene, let me know. I'm always available."

"That reminds me." I wink at Hayley, remembering the night I interrupted his hook-up. "I have to show you the playlist I made up. It's all marching band music."

"I still have to get you back for that," Matt says, closing the door behind him.

Chapter Three

HAYLEY PROMISED, ONCE my profile went live, that there would be plenty of men to choose from when I saw fit to start looking.

Here's the thing: she lied.

All right, maybe she didn't lie per se, but she wasn't exactly on the money.

Sure, there's plenty of men. Tons of men. More men than I could shake a stick at, if I felt like shaking a stick. Which I don't.

But there aren't many who make me sit up and pay attention. Even several hours after finishing the profile, with a decent night's sleep between then and now, I'm not super into this crazy idea of hers. Not when I look at my pool of possibilities.

Don't get me wrong. They're all cute enough—for the most part. They all seem interesting.

None of them do it for me, is all.

"You're not doing this for anything long-term. Don't forget that," she reminded me before leaving the apartment last night—or rather, this morning. We stayed up pretty late, polishing the profile while finishing off a bottle of wine. "Have fun. Experiment. You could even create an amalgam, you know? One main character in your new book who shares traits with a handful of men."

A handful of men. I'm pretty sure she's conducting a social experiment on the side, seeing how many men I can date without picking up a disease. Or a stalker.

I'd rather stick to one man, if at all possible, even if I know darn well my editor would be on Hayley's side in this. There are certain lines I don't want to cross, and that's one of them. Besides, I can barely handle dating one man at a time while working on a book.

There are filters I can click on to narrow down my selection of potential dates, so I figure it's a good idea to do that first.

"Age range," I mutter, leaning in to look at my choices.

There are a bunch of ranges with clicky buttons next to them. Eighteen to twenty-five, twenty-six to thirty-five, and so on.

The first age group seems too young for a doctor, so I leave that one unchecked. It seems to me that twenty-six to thirty-five is a reasonable age range. I don't want to mix in too many tropes and go for a man much older than me.

"Body type," I continue, and now, I'm paying attention.

Granted, the guy doesn't have to be a fitness model on the side. I can write him just as jacked up as my readers expect him to be. But I want to be attracted to him too. I decide to settle on somebody who's fit and healthy. I would think that a young doctor would be fairly fit anyway. Wouldn't he know better than to let himself go?

After I fix my filters, the search results come back at roughly half of the several hundred I was looking at when I first logged in to my account. This is more doable but still overwhelming. I need somebody exciting, somebody interesting, somebody who'll inspire me to write something readers won't want to put down.

It would help if he wasn't a total jerk or, even worse, one of those alpha meatheads some readers are nuts about. I can write him as an alpha male, no problem. I just don't particularly feel like dealing with a *my way or the highway* type in real life.

Only there's no way to tell whether a guy is or isn't that sort just by looking through his dating profile. It's a shame there's no filter to help weed those types out.

It takes a lot of scrolling and the help of a solid breakfast and several cups of coffee, but before long, I've clicked several promising profiles. All the men are cute, all of them either posed with dogs or doing something active. There's a cardiologist on a cliff overlooking a gorge. There's a pediatric specialist on the beach, standing next to a surfboard.

They're not going to expect me to do these things with them, are they? I mean, I can hurt myself just by getting out of bed in the morning. I don't need any help.

First things first, I guess. Reach out to them. What am I supposed to say?

"You're a writer," I growl at myself. "Think of something."

What would my heroine, who right now doesn't have a name or even a physical description—really, I need to get moving on this project—say to attract her ideal partner?

Why do I have to go and make things harder for myself? It's like I have a talent for it. What a shame that I can't make a living from it.

Hi there, I type before deleting it. I don't want to look too eager or corny. *Hi,* I settle on. I *found your profile and knew right away that I wanted to reach out to you.*

Okay, that's a good opener. Should I include something original to each guy? Like surfer boy, for instance. Should I say something about surfing? No, since I don't know the first thing about it. Maybe that's what I should say—that I've never surfed before but always found it interesting.

No. Even though it's true I do find surfing to be really interesting, I just know that if I ever tried it, I would end up drowning. Maybe that's a little too negative, but what can I say? I know myself.

Plus, what happens if he asks me to go surfing with him? I can't help but cringe at the very thought of trying to balance on a board with the ocean rushing under me. No, that wouldn't work at all.

I crack my knuckles and shake my hands out, wishing Hayley were here with me. She would know what to say. *How could she leave me alone with this Herculean task before me?* She should know better.

"Blame her all you want," I whisper, my fingers poised over the keys before I start typing again.

I like going to the beach, too, when my schedule grants me enough time for it—though I'm way too clumsy to be much of a surfer. I'm much more comfortable in front of the laptop, where the only drowning I'll do is metaphorically drowning under the weight of a deadline.

No, no. That's dumb. I'm overthinking this. It's probably for the best that Hayley isn't here because she would roll her eyes hard enough that they might fall out of her head.

I take out everything after the word surfer and write this instead: *Please, when you have a chance, check out my profile. I have it set to private, but you should be able to access it now. I look forward to hearing from you.*

Yes, that will have to do. I'm not going to sit here and craft a message for each of these guys since who knows if they'll ever get back to me? It might end up being a waste of time.

Besides, simple is always the best. Isn't that what Maggie tells me time and again—right before she tears a chapter to shreds and removes some of my favorite lines for the sake of tightening up the story? Maybe I tend to lean too far toward wordiness.

I copy and paste what I just typed out into the message form for each individual profile. All that's left is to wait and see whether I get any bites.

After a few minutes of constantly refreshing my browser, it's clear I need something else to distract myself. If these men are doctors, I'm sure they are super busy, and don't have the time to check their dating profile constantly. They're probably, you know, riding into the ER on a wheeled gurney, doing chest compressions on a dying patient while shouting orders to the doctors and nurses around them.

I may watch slightly too much TV.

I have to get up. *Does my fridge need cleaning? Could I stand to do a load of laundry? Sure, why bother writing character profiles when I could spend my time dealing with busywork like chores?*

I'm halfway to the kitchen when a pair of voices out in the hall catches my attention.

It's Saturday, so I wouldn't expect Matt to spend the entire morning working, but this is different for him. Normally, he doesn't keep his overnight visitors around until midmorning—at least, if he ever does, I don't hear them leaving. They're usually more discreet, I guess.

But not this particular girl.

"You're gonna call me, right?" she asks. It

sounds like she's standing right in front of my door.

Ooh, ooh, this could be interesting. I've never witnessed a one-night stand interrogation like this.

I know I shouldn't take glee from this situation.

But that doesn't stop me from tiptoeing to the door, holding my breath, listening hard for anything Matt might have to say in reply. I can practically feel his discomfort.

"I mean, I had a good time with you. But like I said, I'm usually pretty busy."

Lame.

"Who isn't usually busy?" she challenges. She still sounds like she's kidding around, being playful, but it's a fair question. "I'm not asking you for an engagement ring. Just a phone call. I had fun too—and we could have fun again."

The ball's in your court, buddy. I look out into the hall through the peephole in the door.

Matt scored a very pretty girl last night after leaving me and Hayley to our work. In fact, if I didn't know any better, I would say he chose a girl who looks a lot like my best friend.

Why does my stomach clench a little at the thought? Maybe because it seems pretty creepy, picking up a girl who looks like a girl who just turned him down last night. Not that I think he was seriously interested in Hayley … was he? I guess I can't put anything past him.

"I'm sure we could, but I'd rather be up-front with you. Instead of leading you on, wouldn't you rather I be honest? It's nothing personal."

Ouch. That's the worst thing he could've said. I don't even know this girl, and I feel sorry for her. For a split second, I have half a mind to fling the door open and give him a piece of my mind. But that would probably be the most awkward thing ever, and since I probably will have to see him again at some point in my life, I keep my mouth shut.

"Nothing personal? Cute. Maybe grow up a little and let go of your commitment phobia, okay?" she scoffs, looking him up and down before tossing her head and turning away. Her heels click against the floor and then against the stairs as she stomps her way down.

Now, I have a clear view of Matt, who's dressed in nothing but a pair of low-slung jeans. Even now, with my nose wrinkled in distaste because he said such a jerky thing, I can't help but appreciate his chest and arms and just about everything else. Darn hormones.

He leans against the doorframe, eyes sliding shut as he lets out a long, slow breath.

I almost feel bad for him now. Not just because of the awkward situation he was just in, but because he's so dead set against being involved with somebody in a real way.

It's almost enough to make me angry actually. He likes to pretend he's too busy for anything real or solid, but I know a man who truly is too busy to be in a relationship. His life is nothing like Blake's.

It's just a silly excuse used by a silly boy who wants to have fun but doesn't want any of the responsibility that comes with devoting himself to somebody. I can't help but click my tongue in disappointment.

His eyes open.

He fixes them on my door.

No, not on my door. On the peephole. He's staring straight at me. I press my lips together, holding my breath, afraid to so much as blink and give myself away somehow.

All he does is raise an eyebrow, lowering his chin a little like he's acknowledging me, and then he steps back and closes the door.

Chapter Four

Why do I feel like I'm the one who has to make this work? I text Hayley from the back of the car currently speeding its way through Manhattan, heading for the restaurant where my first doctor date is about to take place.

Xavier—a great name, the perfect name for a romance hero—is a cardiologist at Mount Sinai. He is thirty-four, loves playing basketball with friends when his schedule permits, and is a sucker for romantic comedies.

Okay, even I don't believe that last part. I want to believe there's a perfect guy out there in the world, one who isn't afraid to admit he's a fan of things that are supposed to be strictly for women, but his supposed love of that genre strikes me as pandering.

He wants to make it look like he's into the same sort of things I'm into. Not exactly the worst thing in the world. The guy is trying.

Though if he thinks I'm not going to ask for the name of his favorite romantic comedy, he has another thing coming.

Hayley texts me back. *Maybe because you are? I mean, we're modern women. The onus isn't completely on the man anymore.*

Why did I think you would be any help? I text, anxious. *Aren't you supposed to tell me how gorgeous and sparkling and witty I am and how stupid he'll be if he doesn't see those things?*

The fact that she replies at first with a string of laughing until I cry emojis doesn't go a long way toward making me feel any better. She follows it up with, *Why bother? You already said all those things yourself. Go and have fun and don't put so much pressure on this one single date. That's a surefire way to ruin any chance that things will go well—and I'm telling you this from experience.*

Yes, even a goddess like my best friend has had some truly disastrous dates.

She's right. If I go into it with expectations and pressure, there's no chance things will go well. This is supposed to be fun, isn't it?

He's waiting outside the restaurant. I recognize him from his picture. At least he was accurate with that. I know some people tend to choose photos that don't look much like the way they look now. But Xavier is just as tall, dark, and handsome as he is in his profile pic.

I step out of the car, glad I chose a slightly fancier outfit for our dinner. My gauzy blouse and pencil skirt are a step up from what I'd normally wear on a first date—a little more formal, but this is a pretty formal sort of restaurant.

Xavier's wearing a dark suit and tie and carrying a single red rose. I try not to think of Blake when I see it. He used to love buying me roses.

My gaze travels over his face. Immaculately groomed but not to the point of fussiness. He has a nice, healthy tan, too, and a rugged look to his features that contrasts with his impeccable appearance.

"Xavier?" I ask. "I'm Kitty."

His brows lift as he takes half a step back, like he needs his space to get a good look at me. "Wow, I wasn't expecting to be bowled over."

Very nice, very nice. He's scored a point.

"Thanks." I smile, ducking my head a little.

"Seriously, you're gorgeous." He doesn't bother lowering his voice either, so everybody who walks past knows what he's thinking.

"Okay, you're making me blush," I murmur, and it's the truth. I'm surprised my hair hasn't gone red.

"Sorry. It's just that I haven't met many women who've knocked me out the way you just did." He thrusts the rose my way. "For you. Now, I wish I'd bought a lot more."

"This is beautiful," I assure him. "And more manageable during dinner." Yes, I'm nothing if not practical.

We go into the restaurant, and I note how careful he is to open the door for me, how he keeps glancing down at me while we wait to speak to the host behind the podium. It's a Thursday night, so the restaurant isn't as crowded as it might be on the weekend, but there are still people waiting for their tables.

"Is everything okay?" I ask.

He looks sheepish when he grins. "Sorry—again. You have no idea how different you are from some of the women I've met."

Okay, maybe this loses him a point. Nobody wants to hear about their date's exes.

"I'm sure I'm just like most of them in a lot of other ways." I shrug. I then look around, trying to find something else to talk about that doesn't involve me. "I've always wanted to come here. When you suggested it, I figured it was a good sign."

"They have some of the best seafood in the city," he praises before stepping up to speak to the host.

While he's distracted I have a chance to study him. He carries himself well with the sort of commanding energy I would expect a doctor to possess. Then again, what do I know?

Other than when I was sick as a kid, most of my experience with doctors comes from what I've seen on TV, and I can't imagine much of that being true to life.

I don't know what he says to the man behind the podium, but whatever it is, it gets us seated right away. There's no shortage of frustrated muttering coming from the others who've been waiting since before we arrived, but Xavier waves it off.

"I come here fairly often," he explains when I shoot him a puzzled look.

Hmm. The host didn't look like he was thrilled to see Xavier standing there, to be honest. Not the way I'd expect someone to treat a favorite regular. But it worked.

"Good thing because I'm starving," I confess. Maybe that's not the coolest thing for a girl to say on a date, but I've never had much patience for pretending. If I'm hungry, what's wrong with saying I'm hungry? I'm a human being. If I don't eat, I'll die.

"Just about everything here is perfection," he assures me, pushing the chair in behind me as I take a seat.

A gentleman.

"I'll keep that in mind." I grin when he sits. "Thank you for asking me out tonight. I guess your schedule must get pretty busy, being a cardiologist."

"It can be, but I make it a point to take my free time seriously," he explains. "You don't know how many patients I've seen over the years who've led fairly healthy lives aside from one thing." He holds up a single finger.

"What's the one thing?"

"Overwork. It's just as dangerous as anything else, if not more so, especially when a person works a stressful job. That sort of lifestyle takes its toll. We might not be able to see it on the outside, but you can't lie to your body."

"I'll be sure to remind my editor of that the next time she gets on my case," I offer with a grin.

He chuckles, revealing a dimple in his left cheek. I'm a sucker for a guy with dimples, I have to admit. "Do you need me to provide a note, just in case she's not convinced?"

"I'll keep you posted," I promise with a laugh.

Okay, a sense of humor. Now that we're past the awkward first moments of our date and he's not staring at me like a serial killer imagining what he'll look like while he's wearing my skin as a mask, he seems like a nice guy.

"So"—he leans in a little after we order a bottle of wine, his eyes sparkling in the light thrown off by a candle in the center of the table—"you're a romance writer, huh?"

"Wow, you managed to wait this long before asking about what I do for a living." I wink. "That has to be a record."

"Sorry, I don't mean to offend you."

"No, I'm not offended. Sorry, sometimes, my humor comes off the wrong way. Which is why I'm not a comedienne. And I mean it; usually, people practically jump on me when they find out what I do for a living. I don't know why."

"It's interesting." He shrugs. "It's different. You don't meet a romance writer every day."

"Maybe you do, and you just don't know it," I

suggest with a raised eyebrow. "I mean, some of us get a lot of grief over what we do for a living, so we choose to keep it to ourselves in mixed company. Most people don't take us seriously."

"I don't see why. The romance industry is insanely popular, isn't it? What are the figures I read? Over a billion dollars were spent last year alone on romance novels?"

Another point in his favor.

"You did your research."

"I thought it was the least I could do since I had no idea what it meant to be a writer for a living."

"Should I have researched cardiology?"

We share a laugh over this, and I'm already feeling really good about him. I can see writing him into a book. The tall, dark, and handsome cardiologist who literally makes the heroine's heart go pitter-patter.

Yes, I know how corny that is. I wouldn't write that. At least, not anymore, not now that my editor wants me to participate in a three-way for the sake of my career.

"I'm a pretty laid-back guy in general," he tells me over wine. "When I'm not working, I like to go running, and I swim at the local club."

Yes, he definitely takes care of himself. I would like to see him out of that suit, and it's not the wine leading me to think that way.

"I'm surprised you can find the time."

"I make the time. I believe that's what a person

has to do or else the rest of the world will tell them what to do instead."

"You're so right," I agree, Maggie's image floating around in the back of my mind.

I'm only out with him because of what she told me to do, because I have to date around for the sake of refreshing my career. He doesn't need to know that, of course. Besides, for once, being told what to do has worked out in my favor since he's bordering on dreamy.

"To taking control of our time," he announces, raising his wineglass.

I lift my glass with a smile, reaching across the table to touch it to his.

And somehow manage to light my sleeve on fire in the process.

"No, no, no!" I whisper, batting at my sleeve, dropping the wineglass and sending chardonnay spilling across the table and onto Xavier's suit.

He pushes back from the table with a cry of surprise while I pour the contents of my water glass over my arm.

By now, everybody in the restaurant is watching. Xavier is cursing to himself just loud enough for me to hear, mopping the wine off his suit while I check my arm for burns.

When a server comes over to see if everything's okay, Xavier barks, "Does it look like everything is okay?"

"I'm fine," I whisper, and that's partly true. I

managed not to burn my arm. But something tells me our date is over. I've never seen anybody get so upset over a white wine stain.

Finally, he looks up at me. "Did you burn your arm?" he asks while mopping wine from his jacket.

I shake my head, almost too embarrassed to speak.

"I'm more than happy to pay for the dry cleaning," I finally get out.

"I don't need you to do that," he sighs, sounding about as disgusted as a person would if they found a roach crawling across the floor of the restaurant.

"I really am sorry. I'm always doing stupid things like that," I confess with a shaky laugh. "Good thing I'm out with a doctor, huh?"

He stares at me, blinking in silence for a painful moment before understanding dawns in his dark eyes. "Right. Sure."

Yep, I was right. The date is over.

Chapter Five

"AT LEAST THIS date is just for coffee," Hayley offers as I'm getting ready to meet up with the next sucker who found my profile interesting enough to reach out to me.

"True. No chance of there being any candles on the table this time." And since I'm wearing cute but casual clothes, as I think a coffee date warrants, there's no chance of me ruining yet another expensive blouse.

"Hey, you got a meal out of it," she points out, ever helpful.

"Yeah, but I couldn't remember a single thing I ate if you held a gun to my head and demanded I tell you about it," I grumble. "Things were so tense; I could barely chew, much less enjoy anything I was eating."

"Maybe you can write that into a book someday," she offers.

"I'd better or else the entire thing was for nothing more than my mortification."

Seriously, he barely spoke another word to me. It would've been easier if we had ended things the way I'd figured we would, but instead, Xavier had insisted on being seated at another table with fresh linens. Like it was the principle of the thing.

"Well, maybe he was bitter because he had gone to all the trouble of making time for you and ended up with wine on his jacket because of it." Sarcasm practically drips from her voice.

Clearly, she does not have a very high opinion of Dr. Xavier. Granted, I didn't exactly go out of my way to paint a pretty picture.

"Lesson learned," I announce, deciding on a snug tank top and a thin cardigan, paired with jeans and sandals. "First dates should always be casual. We can get to know each other a little bit before going out to a nice place where I might set the entire restaurant on fire while making a toast."

"Yeah, there isn't much damage you could do in a coffee shop," Hayley agrees.

"Thanks for always making me feel better." I snicker before ending the call.

I only have a few minutes to hustle to the coffee shop. I picked one just around the corner from my building, so I don't need much time to get there.

Sean, the man I'm meeting, is a thirty-two-year-old pulmonologist. Aside from the fact that he made a joke about taking my breath away while the two of us chatted back and forth over the app, he seems like a cool guy. And it's not like I've never made a bad joke in my whole life either. He enjoys skiing in the winter and has a time-share in Vail.

Again, sports are not my friend. I run the risk of setting myself on fire simply by going to dinner. The last thing I need is a pair of skis on my feet while I'm hurtling down the side of a mountain. But the idea of going to Vail for a long weekend and getting cozy by the fire sounds perfect to me.

First things first though. Meeting him face-to-face and getting through the first date without making a complete fool of myself.

I can spot him right away. He's seated at a high-top table by the window, wearing blue scrubs that set off his reddish-brown curls. I wave a little as I walk past since there's a look of recognition on his face when he sees me.

"Sean?" I ask, walking up to the table. "I'm Kitty."

"Hi, Kitty." He has a winning smile and an easygoing way about him, which I find incredibly appealing right off the bat. He doesn't have that serious *I own the world* attitude Xavier had. "I just got off work and was dying for caffeine. I hope you don't mind that I ordered for myself before you got here."

"Not at all—though, jeez, I feel bad for making you come out after you just finished working."

He flashes another easy smile. "No problem. Believe me, I didn't want to miss the opportunity to meet you in person. Can I go get you something?"

I fire off an order, just a simple latte and a blueberry muffin, and then I take a seat while he goes up to the counter. This gives me the chance to observe him, the way he interacts with people. That was something I should've taken closer note of with Xavier—how he treated people. He was a little dismissive toward the host at the restaurant—something I didn't pay much attention to at the time—and he was downright nasty to the server who only wanted to make sure we were okay.

I know by now that how a person treats wait-staff is a good indicator of how they'll treat just about anybody else in their life.

In this respect, Sean scores an A+ across the board. He's all smiles, chatting with the girl at the register, making small talk with a woman who was already waiting for her drink. She chuckles at something he said. By the time he drops a five-dollar bill into the tip jar, I'm very glad he decided to come out with me this morning.

There's another thing I've learned: generous people are often generous in bed. Granted, it's not like I've ever conducted a scientific study into this theory, but it just makes sense.

"My lady, your caffeine and muffin." He places both on the table and then sits across from me.

"Thank you. I can definitely use the caffeine," I tell him.

"Long night? I guess a romance writer has to be out and about, getting inspiration."

"Don't get the wrong idea about me," I warn him. "Like I said in my profile, I'm usually too busy working to do much of anything else. It's rare for me to date."

"I was only teasing. Sorry, I guess it came off the wrong way. I don't do much dating myself. There just doesn't seem to be a lot of time."

"We're both lucky to have technology on our side, huh?" I offer.

"I'm feeling lucky right now since you mention it." He grins, looking me up and down with an appreciative smile.

"So, you're a pulmonologist. That's so interesting, especially to me."

He starts turning his cup in his hand. "Why especially to you?"

"I had pneumonia as a kid. It was pretty serious. I spent, gosh, at least three weeks in the hospital, out in Brooklyn. After that, I saw a pulmonologist regularly for a couple of years, just to be sure there wasn't any lasting damage."

"Yes, that makes sense. Especially with children. The lungs are still developing." He takes a sip from his cup before clearing his throat. "So, what else do you like to do for fun? Besides dating through the site?"

Of course he doesn't want to talk about his work while he's out with a stranger for the first time. He just got off a shift on top of that, so I'm sure he's doubly uninspired to discuss his career.

"You know, now that you ask, I don't do much for fun."

He scoffs, though I can tell he's joking, his warm blue eyes twinkling a little. "Come on. A beautiful girl in the middle of Manhattan? You can't tell me you don't have fun."

"I have to be honest. The last several years have been about nothing but work—for the most part. I spend a lot of my time writing or researching online. My schedule can be so crazy, I don't even go shopping in person. I have to order everything online since the stores are usually closed by the time I'm finished writing. I pretty much feel like a troll living in a cave most of the time."

He laughs kindly, nodding like he understands. "There are times when I leave the hospital and I don't remember what day it is. It doesn't make relationships very easy."

"See? There you go. It's the same thing for me. Granted, a lot of it is self-imposed on my part, but deadlines are deadlines. And honestly, there are days when the words just won't flow. But I don't know they're not going to flow, so I'll sit there for hours on end and force myself to write something, anything."

"Numerous best sellers can't be wrong." He winks before draining his cup. Maybe that's why he seems a little jittery. He basically poured a large latte down his throat in record time.

The fingers of his free hand tap against the tabletop, which, frankly, is starting to get a little annoying. But I can ignore it. Everyone feels a little nervous on a first date even if it's a totally casual thing like this.

"Yes, but my good luck seems to have run out. In fact," – I lean in, arms crossed on the tabletop – "that's a major reason I've started making it a point to date. I figured I should get that out of the way so that you know. Not that I'm going to put you in a book or anything, but you never know." I make it a point to grin just so he knows I'm joking.

"I'm lost," he admits with a grin of his own. "What does dating have to do with your luck running out?"

"I need more life experience when it comes to dating and romance. Readers aren't interested in your run-of-the-mill boy-meets-girl scenario anymore—at least, that's what my editor tells me. My last book tanked, to put it mildly."

"I'm sorry to hear that." Still, he shrugs. "Though it led to you reaching out to me, so I guess I can't be too upset. No offense."

"None taken."

He's a lot of fun, I can tell. I've barely stopped smiling since he sat down.

Though, to be honest, I'm not feeling a spark. Maybe it's the constant tapping of his fingers against the table or the way his other hand is still turning the empty cup around and around.

Or it could be the way his eyes keep sliding away from me, out the window.

"Are you looking for somebody?" I ask, following the direction of his gaze. I don't know what I expect to see, but there's nothing out there but cars and people and buildings.

"Sorry, sorry. I'm distracted. It was a long night." He stretches, which comes as a relief since it means he can't tap out the entire 1812 Overture on the tabletop.

"It must be so stressful," I murmur. "I mean, all I do is write. It's not as easy as people think it is, but it's not the same as helping to save a person's life. I doubt I could ever do your job."

He chuckles at this, waving a hand. "It's not the way you see it on TV."

My Spidey sense is tingling, but I don't know why. He's stopped making eye contact. *Did I say something wrong?* He's probably regretting coming out with me when he's so tired from working all night. I'd regret it if I were in his shoes, I bet.

When his phone rings, I offer to step away for a minute. It couldn't have come at a better time since I'm thinking this isn't going anywhere and I need to come up with a reason to bring an end to it. Something about him isn't sitting well with me, and it's not only the fact that I don't feel even the tiniest spark.

How's it going? Hayley's text is waiting for me when I duck into the ladies' room.

Not so good. I feel like he's uncomfortable and skittish. Maybe he has a girlfriend, and he's worried she'll walk past and see us.

She sends me a laughing emoji, followed by: *Would you be upset if he had a girlfriend?*

It doesn't take more than a half-second's thought to come up with an answer. *No. I'm not feeling any attraction. He's cute but more of a friend type. Not a boyfriend.*

I can always rely on her for a healthy dose of perspective. *And not a hot, sexy, throw-you-on-the-bed and screw-your-brains-out type? Since that's sorta what you're supposed to be looking for.*

Right. I can't lose sight of my goal. This makes me feel icky. I'm starting to think I'll never get this second book written.

Don't blame this on him or anybody else. Whether you write the book or not is completely up to you, she retorts.

Again with the perspective. It's like being best friends with a drill sergeant.

He has to be off the phone and wondering where I am by now, so I hurry to fix a smile on my face that I don't quite feel before leaving the restroom. Before I even see him, I can hear his tense conversation over the light, cheerful music playing over the shop's speakers.

"I told you if you covered for me this morning, I'd cover for you this afternoon. We had a deal," he whisper-shouts. "No, you don't get to change your mind. I know it's busy. I'll be there in fifteen minutes, okay? Yeah, I owe you, fine. Just get back in there before somebody notices we're both gone."

It's only then that he looks up to find me watching, arms folded, waiting for an explanation. No wonder he seemed so skittish and uncomfortable. He's been lying about something, and I'm starting to understand what it is.

He opens his mouth to speak, but I'm too quick for him. "What do you really do for a living, Sean?" I ask, sitting across from him again. "For real this time."

He sighs, rubbing his temples like he's the one with the headache after all this runaround. "Nobody wants to go out with an orderly. Not a girl like you anyway."

An orderly pretending to be a specialist. I guess I've seen worse.

"Who says?"

He lowers his brow. "You mean, you'd still wanna go out with me if you knew I wasn't a pulmonologist?"

No, but not for the reason he's thinking. I'm looking for a doctor because that's who I'm writing about, but I'm not about to go into that with him.

"It doesn't matter. What matters is the part where you lied on your profile. What do you expect? For a girl to laugh off the way you lied from the beginning? That's not a good way to start things off."

"I know. I thought if I could get a foot in the door …"

"It doesn't work that way. I'm sorry you felt like you had to lie," I say, standing and slinging my purse over one shoulder. "Change your profile—

unless you want to keep having this conversation over and over."

"I'm sorry," he offers with a shrug. "I really wanted you to like me."

My heart softens, and I place a hand on his arm. "I know. And the thing is, I would have liked you just fine, though I think we'd make better friends. I'm sure there's a girl out there who'd love to date an orderly. I mean, it really doesn't matter in the end what you do for a living. Does it?"

He snorts. "Yeah. You keep telling yourself that when you're looking for the next doctor to hook up with."

Well, there goes that. I guess I don't have the luxury of the moral high ground when, really, I'm just as much of a liar as Sean is. Not that I'd lie about my career, but I'm still a liar. I'm still using whoever I end up going out with.

At least I can use this as a scene in my book.

Which I really do need to start writing.

Chapter Six

It's amazing how quickly bad things descend on us.

We can be minding our own business, coming in from a walk through the park after a crummy date and actually feeling pretty decent in spite of that. We can be feeling happy about getting a few minutes of sunshine rather than being stuck inside in front of a computer.

And then—bam!—something happens, and everything gets thrown out of whack.

In this particular instance, my something comes in the form of an overeager dog whose owner drops the leash within moments of my footsteps sounding on the stairs. All of a sudden, there's a golden retriever barreling toward me.

"Phoebe!" I gasp in surprise, jumping to the side so she can get past without knocking us both down the stairs.

But she wants me. She doesn't want to get away from Matt. She just wants to say hello.

And she won't take no for an answer.

By the time Matt reaches the top of the stairs,

calling out for the dog, she's managed to wrap her leash around my right ankle while she paws at me with her front legs, trying to lick my cheek.

"Phoebe, down!" he commands.

She obeys.

But sadly, she pulls on the leash when she does. The one around my ankle. And before I know it, I'm tripping down four stairs while trying not to squash her on the way down.

"Son of a biscuit!" I cry out when my ankle twists and pain shoots up my leg. Tears immediately spring to my eyes and land on my cheeks, which Phoebe is all too happy to lick away.

"No, no. Oh God, I'm sorry." Matt's by my side in an instant, crouching on the landing. "What happened? What hurts?"

"My ankle," I groan. When he reaches for it, I slap his arm away. "No! Don't touch!"

"I have to get the leash from around it," he insists, swatting my hand back. "Relax. Breathe slowly. Getting upset is only going to make it feel worse."

"Thanks, Doctor," I mutter before a fresh bolt of pain shoots up my leg at his touch.

"Leave it to you to be snarky, even now," he sighs, unwinding the leash. He's being very gentle at least. "I'm so sorry this happened. First, I dropped my keys on the floor. Then, I dropped the leash when I was going for the keys."

"And you made fun of me for dropping my

wallet last weekend," I remind him through clenched teeth. Already, my right ankle looks bigger than my left. Just my stinking luck.

He shakes his head, scowling. "You need to go to the hospital and get this checked out."

"No, I don't."

"You do. It could be broken."

"I doubt it. I broke my wrist before. It hurt way more than this, and I heard something break. I didn't hear a break this time."

Though frankly, who could have heard anything with Phoebe's heavy, excited breathing?

She takes another lick of my cheek, and I can't help but melt a little when I look into those innocent brown eyes. "It's okay, honey," I whisper, scratching her behind the ears.

"No, it's not okay. Bad girl." Matt takes the leash, standing. "She needs to go, which is why I was taking her out. But once we're back, I'm taking you to the hospital."

"You're not." Only I can't stand or put any weight on my right foot without sheer agony exploding through my ankle.

"I am. Just sit here. Stay put. I mean it." He deposits me on the second step before thinking twice. "No. You should keep it elevated." He then turns me to the side, so my legs are stretched out along the stair's length, and he puts my right foot on the next step up. "Don't move."

"I won't," I groan before he goes running downstairs with Phoebe's leash firmly in hand.

He looks pretty shaken up. I wonder if he's afraid I'll sue or something. I'd never do anything like that. Not even if I was really, truly mad at him. It's nobody's fault.

These things tend to happen to me all the time.

He's back in record time. "Sorry that took so long," he gasps, and I notice he's flushed and sweating like the two of them ran out to the park and back.

"It didn't take long," I point out. "I think you set a record."

"Do you need me to grab anything from your apartment before we go?"

"You're going to make me get this looked at, aren't you?" I huff. Like I had nothing better to do today. "I'd be more than happy to spend the day on the couch with ice on my ankle."

He scrubs a hand over his hair, mussing it. If I wasn't in so much pain, his attitude might actually be endearing.

"Yeah, and I'd spend the whole day worrying whether you were seriously hurt. And what happens if you need something? Knowing you, you'd get up and try to get it for yourself."

"What else am I supposed to do? Rot and die in the same place because I twisted my ankle?"

He glares at me in response, and my heart softens just a little.

"I have my wallet and phone in my purse, of

course. A girl can't go out without ID, just in case."

"For once, you show good sense." Oof, not the time to go insulting me, but he's already stepping over me and guiding the dog to do the same. "I'll be right back."

Funny, if this were any other situation and he were any other man, I wouldn't mind climbing on his back and letting him carry me down the stairs. I might even enjoy wrapping my arms around his shoulders, might get a little shiver from his hands gripping my thighs.

But he's my annoying neighbor and I'm me, and my ankle is screaming at me, so the whole thing strikes me as ridiculous and embarrassing.

ONCE HE GETS Phoebe safely in his apartment, he barrels back down the stairs, picks me up, and carries me outside.

And it's not as romantic as I imagined. More utilitarian.

And embarrassing.

"You can put me down," I hiss in his ear as he's looking around for a cab.

"And have you hop around on the other foot and probably twist that ankle, too, knowing you?" he asks, hailing an approaching car. "Ow! Don't kick me."

"Don't be a jerk then," I retort.

We're still bickering when we reach the ER, which is chock-full of people looking for help. One glance at us, with me on Matt's back and struggling not to cry from the pain, gets me into triage in no time. Before I know it, we're in a curtained-off alcove, waiting to be seen.

"Your name?" a nurse asks when she sweeps into the alcove, looking at the ankle Matt insisted I prop up on a pillow he had taken from a cabinet next to my bed.

"Kathryn Valentine."

She nods like I got the question right. Of course I did. It's my name.

"And you fell?"

"Yeah, down the stairs in my apartment building."

She nods again, looking over what I guess is the information I've already provided. "And you're the boyfriend?" the nurse asks with a sudden sharpness in her voice, glancing up at Matt from her clipboard.

*Oh. Is that why they took me in so quickl*y? Because they think this is a much deeper issue?

We exchange a look of horror.

"Oh, no, no," we both stammer, shaking our heads. "No, we're not together like that."

"I'm her neighbor," he explains.

"He made me fall, but he's not my boyfriend," I add, my voice almost overlapping with his.

"You made her fall?" the nurse asks—no, she *demands* an answer.

"No!" His eyes go wide.

I finally get what it means to look like a deer in headlights because he definitely has that whole terrified thing going on.

"His dog did it. I'm sorry. I should've been clear," I explain. My cheeks are red hot, and it's no wonder. "He didn't have a grip on the dog's leash, and when she heard me coming up the stairs, she got excited and came running. I got tangled up in the leash and fell down a few stairs. That's what happened."

"I didn't lay a hand on her," he adds.

"He didn't," I insist, giving him a look that I hope sums up how sorry I am for making it look like he was the one at fault. "It was his big idea for me to come in. I didn't want to, but he made me."

She's clearly not convinced. "Okay ..." Her eyes move from Matt to mine, locking in with an intense stare.

"Trust me. We're not dating. We're barely even friends." I shrug. Matt lets out a little snicker but doesn't say anything. "We only live across the hall from each other, is what I'm saying. He didn't do anything to cause this."

"All right," she sighs. "The doctor will be in shortly to see you."

"Thank you," I whisper before gulping, looking at Matt.

He's pretty much turned into a statue. A statue with a very angry scowl.

"You made it sound like this was some sort of

domestic thing," he mutters when we're alone.

"I know! My mouth got away from me."

"That wouldn't be the first time," he growls. "I don't know why I'm surprised. Did it ever occur to you that a man bringing a woman in with an injury might set off red flags?"

"No!"

"Yeah, well, now, you know how things work." He runs his hands through his hair, and the sight of how they tremble is what makes me feel about two inches tall. He was truly scared for a minute.

"I'm really sorry," I whisper. There's pressure behind my eyes as tears well up. "I really am. I would never let you take the fall like that."

"I know," he sighs. "It was a mix-up. No big deal. It's just that I feel bad enough about having to bring you here at all, and all of a sudden, I'm defending myself to a nurse. I guess Phoebe's not as well-trained as I thought she was."

"Maybe I have an effect on her." I shrug with a tiny, tentative smile. So long as he's not completely furious. "You could teach me a few words to use when I see her that might calm her down. Whatever it is you say to get her to listen."

"Hmm. Not a bad idea," he admits.

"But I don't hold it against you," I make sure to say. "I don't. It's not your fault. These things happen. To me, most of the time," I add with a smirk.

"You do have a habit of hurting yourself, don't

you?" He arches an eyebrow. "Maybe I need to take out a special insurance policy to protect myself, living across the hall from a walking disaster."

"Okay, hang on a sec. I wouldn't go quite that far."

"When's your birthday? Maybe I'll get you a bubble to live in."

"Shut up."

"How much do you think it would cost to line the walls and floors with bubble wrap?"

"How much would it cost for me to wrap you in plastic and throw you in the Hudson River?"

"Have I interrupted something?"

We both turn our heads in surprise at the sound of a third voice. Neither of us was paying attention when the doctor entered the curtained-off alcove.

The sight of him knocks the wind from my lungs. He looks like he just stepped out of a superhero movie—or at least a wrestling show. He's got to be six foot five with a head of thick, wavy brown hair held back from his face in a low ponytail. I'd love to know how the heck he found a white coat to fit over his bulging shoulders and chest.

"N-no," I stammer. Jeez, I'm blushing—no, I'm flushed, and it's spreading all over my body. It would be bad enough for that to happen if I were alone with Dr. Hunky, but Matt's here to witness it too. "It's okay."

His clear green eyes move back and forth between Matt and me before his sensuous—yes, sensuous, I said it—mouth tugs upward at one corner. "What have we here then? Miss Valentine, is it?"

"It is." My hand is probably sweaty, but I can't ignore the hand he extends for a shake. It engulfs mine, bringing to mind an adult taking a child's hand. Not the sexiest place my thoughts could've gone, but that's okay. Now is not the time for sexy thoughts.

"And you are?" He turns to Matt with a smile.

"Matt Ryder. The neighbor whose dog caused this," Matt explains, wanting to get that part out there before there are any wrong ideas floating around. Again.

"These things happen." The hunky doctor shrugs.

God, how do the seams on his coat stay together with all those muscles moving around underneath? Especially in the shoulder region, though his biceps are enormous too.

"I'm Dr. Jake Becker."

Jake Becker. Jake. Yes, I can imagine moaning his name, gripping those obscenely massive shoulders while he—

Get a grip on yourself.

I have to dig my nails into my palms to bring my thoughts back into focus, though a simple move of my sore foot would've done the trick. As soon as the doctor places even a soft touch against it, I wince.

"Sorry about that." Jake frowns. "Let's see what we have here."

He pulls up a stool on wheels and perches on it, positioned … right in front of where I'm lying on the bed. Between my legs. *Holy moly.* I have half a mind to ask Matt if there isn't something else he'd rather be doing right now because the presence of probably the most beautiful man I've ever seen has me feeling all sorts of mixed up and, well, horny. For lack of a better word.

And I'm a writer. I know lots of words. But this is flat-out horniness. Animal lust. I'm practically salivating all over myself.

He's exceedingly gentle as he closes a hand around my lower calf, lifting my leg off the pillow it's been propped up on all this time. "You're looking fairly swollen," Jake murmurs, comparing one ankle to the other.

"Hmm? Oh, yeah." I frown. What an unfortunate choice of words because, now, all I can do is think of other swollen things …

"Can you move it at all?" he asks, his eyes locking with mine and basically shooting an electric current up and down my spine.

I try to move it, grimacing as I do. Pain has a way of wiping away all sexy thoughts.

Still, the doctor's smiling a little. "The fact that you can move your foot at all is a good thing," he assures me, holding my leg with one hand while he presses lightly on my swollen flesh with the tips of his fingers. "I'll send you down for an X-ray to be sure, but it's more than likely nothing worse than a sprain. I know that's bad enough, but right now, it's the best-case scenario."

"Thank you," I breathe. *Why am I thanking him? He didn't do anything.*

"Dr. Becker!" somebody calls out from the hall.

He sighs, reaching into the breast pocket of his superpowered coat. I mean, it has to be superpowered, right? Or else it would shred under the strain of all that muscle. "I'm sorry. We're up to our necks in patients today. Feel free to reach out to me *anytime* if you have any problems." He hands me a card with his name and number.

"Thank you," I breathe again. Jeez, he's going to think I'm a real loser. I can barely string a handful of words together in his presence.

"No problem." He even winks before turning to Matt, shaking his hand again. "And good on you for bringing her in. We should all have decent neighbors like you."

I have to bite my tongue since it's my impulse to be snarky whenever Matt's the topic of conversation. The poor guy has already been through enough today.

Besides, I'm holding what looks like the key to my next book. Granted, I don't know if he's single—he wasn't wearing a ring, but that doesn't mean there's no girlfriend in the picture.

Though, let's be honest, how often does a doctor hand a patient his card when it looks like their issue is nothing worse than a sprained ankle? Why would I need to follow up with him? I can be oblivious when it comes to a lot of things, but even I managed to pick up on that not-so-subtle hint that Dr. Dreamboat wants an excuse to chat again.

"Welp." Matt leans his back to the wall near my feet, folding his arms over his chest. "There I was, beating myself up over what happened to you. All this time, I should've been patting myself on the back."

"What? Why?"

"Because you just met the hero of your next book." He smirks. "Don't forget to dedicate this one to me."

Chapter Seven

"SHOULD I CALL him?" I turn the card in my hand over and over. It's already a little worn around the edges from me handling it so much.

"Oh my Lord, if you don't do it, I will." Hayley laughs. "What's up with you? It's not like you to be so indecisive. Don't tell me I used my entire fifteen-minute lunch break to call you for a supposed emergency, and this is the emergency."

"Do you really only get fifteen minutes?" I whisper, horrified.

"Stick to the subject—and yes, pretty much, I eat while I'm working."

As it is, I can hear her fingers hitting keys while she's speaking. Lord only knows what super-important thing she's typing up.

"I'm sorry. I'll leave you alone." She clicks her tongue like she's annoyed. "No, really," I insist. "I'm not being pissy, if that's what you think. You're right. I'm being indecisive, and that's the last thing I need right now."

"Exactly. You haven't had the best luck so far, and your ankle has you laid up for a few days anyway. So, no chance of meeting up with anybody new until you're up and around. Why not strike while the iron's hot and call him up? You're the cute girl he met yesterday. He'll remember you."

"You think so?"

"I know he will. You're calling him. Right?"

"Right," I groan.

"Today?"

"Today."

"This afternoon?"

"Hayley."

"It has to be this afternoon or else you're going to lose your nerve. I know it. And we'll end up having this same conversation tomorrow, and I'll want to seriously slap some sense into you by then. You don't want me to slap some sense into you, do you?"

"If I can avoid it, I'd rather not."

"There you go." I hear voices in the background. "Gotta scoot. Text me when you call."

She's gone before I can say good-bye. The life of a lawyer.

This leaves me with the doctor's card still clutched in my sweaty palm.

Why am I so nervous about this?

Oh, right. Because he's easily the sexiest man I've ever met in person, and I'm afraid of making myself out to be a total idiot.

But.

I have a book to write.

He's a doctor who gave me his card.

I have a book to write.

He's hot.

I need to know what his skin tastes like.

I have a book to write.

Yes! So I need to know what his skin tastes like.

It's research.

Argh! I can't even pace the apartment with my foot propped up on pillows, the way Matt insisted it be whenever possible. He's been super helpful since he brought me home yesterday and now I'm not sure if he's being nice or worried I'll make his life a living hell. Maybe we can call it even for me blasting the marching band music through the wall.

Since I'm afraid he'll barge in and find me doing something I'm not supposed to do and since I can't really walk anyway, there's nothing but sulking on the couch with my laptop to sustain me in this moment of crisis. I can't even take an old toothbrush to the grout around the bathtub, which is always a calming exercise.

The thing is, I know I'm making way too big of a deal out of this. It's like standing outside myself, looking in. Shaking my head in despair. That part of me knows this will all be over once I make that phone call. Once the ball's in Dr. Sexy's court. And I'll laugh at myself for ever taking this so seriously.

I have to rip off the bandage all at once.

I have to jump in, no matter how cold the water is.

I have to get it over with.

So, I do.

"Don't pick up, don't pick up," I whisper, eyes squeezed tightly shut, fingers crossed. I might stammer my way through a voice mail, but it'd still be easier than this.

"Hello?"

Oh, help me. That deep voice of his. *How did I not notice its rumbling quality yesterday? Because I was too busy holding myself back from humping him like a deranged monkey. Right.*

"Hi. Hello. Uh, Dr. Becker?"

"Speaking." He sounds busy but friendly. Not put out. A good sign.

"This is Kitty Valentine. I saw you in the ER yesterday. The sprained ankle. I'm sure you had a million people to take care of—"

"I remember you," he assures me with a soft chuckle that does things to me. I'm serious. A yearning in my core magically appears at the sound of that chuckle. "Is everything okay? Has the swelling gotten worse?"

It's so unfortunate that he keeps talking about swelling.

"No, it hasn't," I whisper. My throat's suddenly so dry. Darn it, I should've been better prepared for this. A glass of water, a cold shower. Something. "Everything's the way I guess it should be. I wanted to reach out and thank you for how kind you were. I was hurting, but you calmed me down and made me feel better. My neighbor too," I add for some reason I can't imagine.

"I sensed he was upset," he admits. "And I'm glad you feel better, though I didn't do much. If anything, I should apologize for not having the opportunity to check in on you before you were discharged."

"It's not a problem." Though I have to say, my heart sank through the floor when I realized I wouldn't be seeing him again. Just to get one more look at him. *How does anybody get any work done in his presence?*

"Still, I'd like to make it up to you."

Yes. Yes, yes, yes, let's do that. Make it up to me. I have to literally dig my nails into my palm until it hurts, just to center myself enough to respond without giggling like I've lost my ever-loving mind. I mean, he's probably used to women losing IQ points while in his presence, but still.

"How would you do that?" I finally ask once I'm fairly sure I won't giggle like a maniac.

"Well, I was thinking lunch sometime soon. I have this weekend off …"

I have to hold the phone to my chest for a second while I fist pump and repeatedly mouth the word yes. "That would be nice," I agree. "I should be up and around by then, right?"

"There's no reason you can't be—unless you overwork the ankle during the week. Be sure not to overdo it, okay?"

"I'll be sure." *Oh, you bet I'll be sure.* I'll be the best patient he's ever seen and sit on the couch all week and type if that's what it comes to. I'll fester in the same clothes I'm wearing right this very minute. Anything so long as I'm able to make myself presentable for our lunch.

He promises to call with firmer plans later in the week—by Friday at the latest—leaving me with nothing to do but hyperventilate when the call is finished.

My instincts were right on the money for once. I'm not usually good at picking up signals from men, probably because I don't spend a ton of time around them—or frankly, anyone. I wasn't kidding when I called myself a troll during that disastrous coffee date.

Hayley needs to know about this.

We're going to lunch this weekend! I text with shaking hands, even squealing a little.

See? I should've known, she replies.

Known what? I ask.

Given enough time, you were bound to meet a doctor. All you have to do is step outside your apartment, and the odds go way up.

I roll my eyes at this, though she's obviously right.

Now that the most heart-clenching part of my day is done—and I was right; I feel totally relieved and annoyed with myself for hemming and hawing—it's time to dive into character profiles.

This book isn't going to write itself.

Chapter Eight

"WOW. YOU LOOK terrific."

Thankfully the twelfth dress I put on this morning while agonizing over what to wear to a simple lunch date was the right choice.

One look at the magnificent man in front of me is enough to make me forget what I'm wearing and how torturous it was to make a decision. My bedroom might look like a tornado tore through it but since I don't even remember my address right now I'll take the compliment.

Because, holy wow, he is the most jaw-dropping, smoldering man I've ever set eyes on. Even in a polo shirt—light green, which complements the green in his eyes—and a pair of jeans, he's exquisite. I'm not sure I measure up.

Though the way he's looking at me says he doesn't agree. His gaze travels up and down, a smile tugging one corner of that mouth of his.

Jeez, what I wouldn't do to feel that mouth on mine. Focus, Valentine. Try not to get arrested for sexual assault today.

I run my hands over the sundress I finally decided on. "Thanks. I went with flat sandals, so I wouldn't aggravate the ankle."

"I see that." He grins. "Very nice. It spares me the trouble of having to carry you around all afternoon."

"I didn't know that was in the cards. I could always go home and put on a pair of heels."

Oof. Yeah, that was too much.

His eyes widen, brows lifting. "Pardon?"

Crap, crap, crap. "It was supposed to be a joke," I explain with a weak shrug. The idea of being carried around in his absolutely droolworthy arms was over the top.

Only when he flashes a killer grin do I remember to breathe again. "Sorry. I'm a little slow on the uptake. Hey, if you need a lift, I'd be more than happy to offer my services."

Dear Lord, he even flexes his biceps. If he doesn't quit it with that sort of thing, I might need to be carried around after all.

Only it won't be any fun since I'll be unconscious the entire time. There's no way my heart can take this. *Do I need a hormone suppressant or something? Does such a thing even exist?*

The restaurant is trendy but casual, the patio out front chock-full of people trying to take advantage of the beautiful day. When the hostess—who, by the way, looks like she might faint dead away when Jake approaches—suggests we take one of those tables, I agree.

I also manage to sneak a look over my shoulder as we walk away and find her fanning herself behind Jake's back.

Same, girl, I think when we make eye contact.

"I hope you're not a vegetarian," he murmurs when we take a seat against the metal fencing that separates us from the rest of the sidewalk.

"Huh? Why's that?"

"Because the burgers here are to die for. Though you don't look like you've eaten a burger in the last few years," he adds with an appreciative glance over the top of his menu.

"For a doctor, you're not very good at reading people." I wink. Granted, I don't adore the comment about my body, but he was trying to be complimentary. "I practice yoga every day and generally try to keep it healthy, but all bets are off when a worthwhile burger is waved in front of me."

"This is more than worthwhile," he promises.

How is it possible for his smile to be so dazzling? Not like game show–host dazzling. There's nothing false or phony about it. In fact, when he flashes those pearly whites, he manages to look more approachable. Younger. Adorable, in general.

Though my heart still skips a beat because, duh. Muscles. Piercing eyes. Full mouth just begging to be …

I have to raise my menu to hide the blush covering my cheeks. "Anything else you recommend?" I ask in a choked voice.

"The sweet potato fries are excellent too."

I lower the menu just enough to meet his gaze. "You don't look like you've eaten sweet potato fries in the last few years."

"Ah, nicely done." He grins. *Excellent. A man with a sense of humor.* "Point taken. I don't eat like this all the time. I wouldn't have the energy to get through the day if I did. This is a treat—the menu and the company."

Oh, smooth. He's checking all my boxes.

"What do you do when you're not treating hopelessly clumsy girls in the ER?" I ask while we wait for a server.

"Wanna see?" he asks with a gleam in his eye.

I don't know what to make of that gleam, so at first, I'm more tongue-tied than I already was.

It's when he pulls out his phone to show me pictures of two absolutely beautiful huskies that I understand.

"Oh my gosh, they're gorgeous!" I breathe, admiring them.

"By all means," he says, handing me the phone. "That's my folder of dog pics. I … probably take too many of them."

Could he be any more perfect? I'm pretty sure it wouldn't be possible at this point. There's a photo of the dogs running on the beach. One of them in the park and then another. One of the two of them on the floor with Jake in the middle, taking a selfie. He's wearing a goofy, completely joyful smile.

"I'd take endless pictures if I had dogs like them," I admit, handing the phone back. "So, that's how you stay healthy? Running around after them?"

"I do work out in the gym in my building," he admits, "but otherwise, yeah, keeping them walked and exercised is more than enough."

I'm sure. They'd probably pull my arm off if I tried walking them.

"Hi." Our server appears, standing closer to Jake than she needs to.

The poor girl's a little breathless. I can relate to that, and I have to wonder how hard she fought to be the lucky person to take care of our table.

He showers his stunning smile upon her. "Hey."

She doesn't say anything for a moment, satisfied to stare at him. I clear my throat, and that seems to jerk her out of her daze. "Um, I'm Mel. I'll be your server. Can I start you off with something?"

"I think we're ready to order," he tells her before looking to me for confirmation.

"I'm entirely in your hands." I smile before looking up at flustered, panting *Mel. Watch it, babe. He's here with me.*

What's this new side to my personality? It's like being around this man has turned me into a different person, one with the ability to shoot daggers at another woman with my eyes. All because she's as attracted to him as I am.

I'm not normally the possessive type—and seeing as how this is a first date, there's nothing for me to be possessive over. Strange.

Regardless, it seems to work. She snaps out of it for good and takes our order before hurrying off. *Does he have even the slightest idea of the effect he has on women?*

"So …" he continues, resting his massive forearms on the table. There is something so sexy about a man's forearms—at least, there is about his. "What do you do? I don't know anything about you—other than the fact that you claim you're clumsy."

"Painfully clumsy," I admit. "Which is why I don't play a sport or even take dance classes for exercise. Yoga is just about the safest thing I can manage."

"What else though?" he prods, flashing that panty-melting smile. "What do you do for a living?"

Always this question. Well, it's only fair. I already know what he does. "I'm a romance novelist."

His eyes go wide. "You're kidding."

"Not even a little bit."

Yep, here we go. He's going to laugh at me. I mean, I'm only a writer while he's a doctor. All I can do is brace myself for it and then prepare to be dismissed as an airhead.

Instead of laughing, however, he nods. "I knew it. I knew I'd seen your name before. I can't believe I'm having lunch with the famous Kitty Valentine."

Okay, clearly, I have stepped into bizarro world. I blink rapidly, like that's going to help anything. "I can't believe you've heard of me."

"Are you kidding? Manhattan's own Kitty Valentine? Yeah, in case you're wondering, that's how they advertise you at the indie bookstore down the street from my building." He grins while I gape at him in surprise. "I've seen your books in the window before. It's hard to forget a name like yours. Only it said Kathryn on your intake form at the hospital. It was such a busy day, and I didn't put two and two together."

"Here I was, assuming you would laugh at me when I told you what I do."

"Why would I do that?" He's all innocence, too, without even the ghost of a smile, which tells me he's serious.

Now, I feel like I've been put on the spot. I shrug, stammering, while he fixes me with a penetrative gaze, "Because a lot of people think romance writing is a joke. Like all we do is write a bunch of sexy scenes and string them together with a thin plot and the same recycled characters."

"Is that what you do?" Again, he's completely serious.

He has a way of looking at me that makes me feel really, truly seen. It also makes me feel kind of squirmy, like he's studying me. But in a good way—almost anyway.

"No! No, there are no recycled characters in my

books. And until recently, my romance was clean."

"Clean?"

Terrific. I sincerely wish we hadn't gotten on this topic in the first place, but I guess I only have myself to blame. "You know … no sexy times. Just straight-up relationship stuff."

He sits back in his chair, lips pursed. Help me, Lord, he looks even hotter that way. "If anything, I would think that would be even more difficult to write. You have to come up with a relationship for two people that's compelling enough to get a reader to keep reading. They're not picking up your books just to get off." He frowns. "Sorry, that was crude."

"No, it wasn't." Maybe it was a little bit, but I'm too busy being impressed with how quickly he understood the situation to care very much about his choice of words. Besides, it's not like I haven't been fantasizing about doing any number of filthy things to him since the second I laid eyes on him in the ER last weekend.

That's an entire week's worth of fantasizing. It got pretty raunchy. Maggie will be beside herself with excitement when she reads what I've come up with so far.

"You said 'until recently' though," he recalls. "What's that mean?"

Thank goodness our food shows up just now because I need to find a way to broach the subject tastefully. *This is always going to be a minefield, isn't it?* Once we start talking about my career, we're going to have to eventually get to the point where I describe the recent turn of events.

"My editor wants more ... you know ... spiciness. Heat." Like the heat rushing over my skin, making it flush.

"How do you feel about that?" he asks before popping a fry into his mouth.

It takes an act of sheer willpower just to pry my eyes away. I could watch him do just about anything.

He asked a question, right? I have to think hard to remember what it was. "I wasn't super thrilled at first, to be honest. I sort of took it as an insult, though now, I see how immature my reaction was. But I guess all writers feel that way at one point or another. Like even constructive criticism means what they're doing isn't good enough."

"Sex sells, right?" He arches an eyebrow, inserting another fry into that delectable mouth of his. This time, he moves a little more slowly. Deliberately.

I have a feeling his thoughts have taken a turn. They might as well since my thoughts have been in the gutter all week.

"So they tell me," I reply with a coy smile, looking down at my food if only so I can stop staring at him. The burger is enormous, easily enough for two meals. "How am I supposed to fit all of this into my mouth at once?" I ask.

It's not until he starts choking that I realize what

I just said. His face turns bright red, his eyes bulging as he coughs.

"Oh no!" I gasp in horror as he tries to bring up whatever is stuck in his throat. For an instant, all I can imagine is trying to get my arms around him to give him the Heimlich maneuver. It would be like trying to hug a grizzly bear.

It's official. I might as well be registered as a deadly weapon. I just killed a promising young doctor. Cause of death? Asphyxiation due to double entendre.

Except he doesn't die, coughing one last time before clearing his airway.

He takes a long drink of water, shaking his head and waving his hand when I ask if he's all right. "I'm fine. Sorry. That struck me as hilarious. I might look like a grown-up doctor, but most men are dirty-minded teenage boys on the inside."

"So long as I didn't do any permanent damage." I laugh, a little weak.

"Not even close. A little thing like you? I doubt you could do damage if you tried."

"I don't know. I might surprise you."

"I welcome the opportunity to be surprised."

Something tells me we're not talking about choking on a French fry anymore. And that's just fine by me.

Which, naturally, is exactly when the entire thing comes crashing down around me. Because why not?

"Kathryn? Kathryn, my dear!"

I know that voice. I grew up with that voice. Just like I grew up with her calling me by my formal name, no matter how many times Mom had insisted on using my nickname.

I look over Jake's impressive shoulder and find my grandmother walking our way. Somehow, even in the middle of a crowded New York sidewalk, she finds a way to make her voice rise above the bustle.

And as always, she looks absolutely stunning. All bitterness at her terrible sense of timing aside, as I watch her approach, I can't help but hope that I age half as gracefully as she has. Her snow-white hair is artfully arranged in a chic chignon, and I'm pretty sure her sheath dress is Valentino. So is the coat she wears over her shoulders—it's way too warm for a coat, but she didn't put it on for the sake of keeping warm.

"Grandmother, what a surprise!" *Can she tell how completely distressed I am? Can Jake?*

She leans over the railing, kissing both my cheeks before turning to my lunch date. She's wearing her customary sunglasses, big enough to take up half her face, but I can see the way her brows lift in surprise just the same. "And who is this?" she asks, already extending a manicured hand.

"Grandmother, this is a friend of mine. Dr. Jake Becker. Jake, this is my grandmother."

"Cecile Harrington," she clarifies as he stands to

shake her hand. And when he does, she has to tilt her head back to look him in the eye.

"It's a pleasure to meet you." He smiles. "Would you like to join us for lunch?"

Now, it's my turn to nearly choke to death. The concept of my upper-crust grandmother eating at a pub is about as likely as a fish learning to fly. He's only being polite though, and I can tell this impresses her as her smile widens, becoming more genuine.

"Thank you, but I'm on my way to a luncheon, and I'm afraid I'm running late. It was lovely to meet you." She then turns to me, and something about the way her mouth's set tells me there's plenty she wants to say. "Kathryn, darling, I would love it if you paid me a visit tomorrow. I've been meaning to talk to you about some plans on the horizon."

What the heck? Since when does she include me in her plans? I can't help but feel this is a ploy to get as much information out of me as possible, and already, I feel a little twitchy at the thought. "Okay. I can drop by tomorrow."

"Wonderful. I'll have Peter fix up a little lunch for us. Noon sharp." She kisses my cheeks again and waves to Jake before continuing down the street.

"She's impressive," Jake observes with a faint smile as he sits.

Yes, and something tells me she's going to have an ear full for me tomorrow.

Chapter Nine

I TOUCH A hand to the pearls around my neck before raising the other hand, one finger pressed against the doorbell. I can hear it ringing inside the house, and soon, the sound is followed by footsteps.

Peter is practically my grandfather, though as far as I know, he and grandmother have never been together that way. He's been her faithful butler, driver, cook, and companion for pretty much my entire life. And the smile that shines from his lined face tells me he's as happy to see me as I am to see him.

"Miss Kathryn, it's been too long," he chides, ushering me into the foyer.

"How many times do I have to tell you to let the Miss Kathryn thing go?" I tease.

No matter how many times I've asked him to call me plain old Kathryn or, preferably, Kitty—though he never will since grandmother would have a fit—he insists on keeping things formal.

"As always, avoiding the question," he teases right back, though he's much drier about it than I am.

"Peter, come on now. You know how busy I am, writing books my grandmother pretends don't exist." I give him a wink and a grin to soften my words, but there's a heck of a lot of truth in them.

She would rather pretend I do something respectable like, I don't know, live as the wife of a successful man.

"Just the same, you work too hard." He pats my cheek, which is about as close to physical contact as we've ever gotten. From him, this is the same as a warm hug, and I soak it up just like I would if he really were hugging me.

"She's in the sitting room," he informs me. "I'll have lunch ready in a few minutes." I follow him down the hall, taking in the same surroundings as ever. My grandmother doesn't believe in change, though I guess if I lived in a magnificent brownstone on Park Avenue, I wouldn't feel the need to change anything either.

"Kathryn. Punctual as ever." I get the whole double-cheek kiss thing before she sits me down on the silk-covered sofa. "Can I fix you a drink?"

She's not talking about iced tea either.

"No, thank you." I demurely cross my legs at the ankles, the way she's always harping on me to do. "It's a little early for me."

If she gets that I'm making a pointed comment about her drinking habits, she lets it go. She's from the days when people drank a heck of a lot more than they do now. Afternoon cocktails, drinks before dinner, a pitcher of daiquiris while playing cards with the girls.

"Very well. Now, I can ask what's been on my mind since I saw you yesterday." She turns to me, cocktail shaker in hand. "Who was that gorgeous hunk of manhood, and why in the world haven't you locked him down yet?"

"Grandmother …" I warn, rolling my eyes.

"I'm serious, Kathryn. I nearly forgot to breathe! I don't think I've ever seen a man like that in person. And to think, he was having lunch with you!"

"You don't have to sound so astonished," I mutter.

"And a doctor on top of everything else! What does he do in his spare time? Pull small children from burning buildings?" She snorts, pouring her drink into a glass before adding garnish. "I can imagine he's pretty good with his hose."

I'm used to this. On the outside, my grandmother is the picture of elegance, refinement. And for the most part, she's just as she appears to be.

On the inside, however? She has a wild streak a mile wide. And she certainly has no trouble sharing her thoughts with me.

"What I wouldn't give to be your age again," she sighs, shaking her head as she crosses the elegant room. "That man would be tied to my bedposts right this very minute, begging for mercy."

"Grandmother, please."

"Why am I not surprised at your attitude?" she sighs, shaking her head in dismay. "You've always been too prim for your own good."

"I am not either!"

"No?" She sits at the other end of the sofa, fixing me with an appraising look. "Then, you've slept with him?"

"Is this seriously why you asked me to lunch? So we can talk about my sex life?"

"No, there is another reason, but all I've been able to think about since yesterday afternoon is that gorgeous doctor. You're going to blow this, aren't you?"

"Thank you so much for all your faith in me. To answer your question, no, we haven't slept together."

"I thought so."

"I met him a week ago and only because I twisted my ankle and went to the emergency room. He was the doctor who treated me. Jeez Louise, I was laid up most of the week with a sprained ankle! What do you expect me to do?"

"Sweetheart, you might think your grandmother is old-fashioned and behind the times—"

"Trust me, that's not what I think at all."

"But I know the way the world works. If you don't lock him down—and fast—you're going to lose him. They always used to say the way to a man's heart is through his stomach, but I think you and I both know better."

When she wiggles her eyebrows up and down, leaving absolutely no question as to what she has in mind, I find myself wishing I could melt straight through the polished walnut floor.

"It was just a lunch date. We're not picking out our china patterns just yet."

"All the more reason for you to get on the ball," she reminds me, holding my gaze as she sips her martini. Dry, two olives, just like always.

The only reason I can handle the way Maggie talks about sex and men is because I've been hearing it from my grandmother ever since she decided I was old enough to be spoken to this way. She's a very beautiful woman, and she was born into a family where money was never a problem. As such, I'm sure she had more than her fair share of interested men during her single days and even after she married my grandfather, who'd also come from a good deal of money.

He passed away a little more than a decade into their marriage, and I can only imagine how many men have fought and clawed their way over each other in an attempt at getting close to her.

Something tells me she hasn't turned all of them away either. And why should she?

"Aren't you the one who always reminds me that you'd rather shoot yourself in the head than ever get married again? Yet here you are, trying to put me into a marriage with a guy you spent all of ten seconds with yesterday."

She puts on a sour face. "That's different. I have already been married, and I loved your grandfather very much—even if we never agreed with his insistence on managing my money as if I couldn't be trusted. I also had your mother. I had a secure home life. Lord knows I have enough money of my own. And I'm certainly past the point of ever having another child by around thirty years. Why would I want to marry a man now?"

"So you'll have somebody in your life?"

This earns me indulgent laughter.

"Darling, I can have somebody in my life whenever I want. I happen to prefer being able to ask them to go home when I want to be alone, is all."

Even though she drives me crazy and seems to take pleasure in embarrassing me, I want to be her when I grow up.

"All of that is neither here nor there," she sighs, waving a hand. "I want you to bring him to my birthday party. You must."

"Birthday party?"

"Yes, darling! My seventy-fifth! I've never understood this obsession with hiding one's age, to be honest. I've lived nearly seventy-five years and think I ought to celebrate, don't you?"

"I wholeheartedly agree." I also feel like garbage, having forgotten her birthday was even coming up.

It's hard, having nobody else in my life to bring

up things like this in conversation. I'm sure if Mom were still alive, she'd have reminded me of the upcoming day.

She nods firmly. "It will be here, at the house, and I plan on inviting all of my friends. Naturally, you'd be my most honored guest. I know everyone would love to see you; it's been too long."

"That's true. I haven't been to one of your big, swanky parties since you turned seventy."

"Don't say swanky, dear," she chides, wrinkling her patrician nose. "It sounds low-class."

Oh, and complaining that I haven't slept with Jake yet is so high-class?

I have to bite my tongue a little to keep my thoughts on that to myself. "Sure, I'd love to be here." I smile and then, "Though I don't know about Jake."

"Come now. You have to bring him. I want everyone to see him."

"He's not a zoo exhibit, you know."

"You know very well what I mean. My granddaughter's gorgeous doctor boyfriend!" She clasps her hand over her heart like her wildest dream has come true.

"He's not my boyfriend—and he's a doctor in an ER, which means his schedule might not permit him dropping everything and spending an evening here."

"The party is two weeks away. I'm sure he can work something out."

"Spoken like a woman who hasn't worked a day in her life," I sigh.

"Oh, you know I do board and committee work," she reminds me, waving her hand again like this is all nothing more than a lot of silly nonsense. Which, I guess, it sort of is.

"Don't get your hopes up," I implore. "He's probably going to look at this as a trap. Like, a family event after knowing me for a few weeks? And the first week doesn't even count since our first date was yesterday."

"It doesn't matter." She reaches out, shifting my hair over my shoulders with a gentle, loving touch. "You're my beautiful, brilliant Kathryn. You'll come up with something to convince him."

"I wish I had as much faith in myself as you seem to have in me."

"I wish you did too," she murmurs with a soft smile moments before Peter announces that lunch is ready.

Chapter Ten

"I CAN SEE why you call this exercise!" I'm going to have to stretch my arms and shoulders beforehand if Jake ever asks me to help him walk his dogs again.

I have Romulus while he's walking Remus, and they're both extremely strong and full of energy.

I sorta want to recommend whoever Matt used to train Phoebe though. They're not so cool with being told what to do. Or that they need to stop pulling so darn much. Maybe it doesn't matter to Jake since he's basically superhuman, but little old me is getting yanked all over the place.

He finally takes pity on me when we're a few blocks from his apartment. "Let me," he offers, holding out his free hand. "You'll dislocate your shoulder and end up in the hospital again."

I'm not too proud to gladly hand the leash over. "Thanks. I didn't know whether I should say something or not. I don't want you thinking I'm a weakling."

"I would never." He grins.

Good thing he took the leash because I feel weak

all over when he shoots me a look like that.

"I'm so glad you have the afternoon off," I observe, and what an afternoon. It's absolutely dazzling outside, zero humidity and a fresh breeze blowing away any staleness. The sort of day a person wants to spend completely outside if they can. I've already decided to do some writing on the roof of my building later on since the thought of being cooped up inside to do my work makes my heart sink.

"Me too. It means I get to spend a little time with you, Manhattan's own Kitty Valentine."

"You're never going to let me live that down, are you?"

"Hey, better that than the fact that you almost made me choke to death. Maybe I should avoid you out of self-preservation."

"Don't say I didn't warn you." I shrug, giggling. "I'm sort of a disaster. Sometimes, it rubs off on the people around me."

"I'll take my chances," he decides before throwing a protective arm in front of me, keeping me from crossing into a busy intersection. "The light hasn't changed yet."

No, it hasn't. There I go, not paying attention, too busy soaking in the glorious man next to me. Having his arm against my chest is almost worth the possibility of getting hit by a car.

But not quite. I mean, it's an impressive arm, but I would like the chance to feel the rest of him too. I can't very well do that if I'm dead.

"Thanks." I blush. "See? I warned you."

"Looks like I have to keep a close eye on you."

"Looks like you will."

Oh, yes, he can keep as close an eye on me as he wants. I'm not in the market for a stalker, but some light voyeurism wouldn't be out of the question if he plays his cards right.

Note to self: write a scene where the hero's watching the heroine do something sexy.

"There's something I have to ask you." The light changes, and we continue on. At least the dogs knew well enough to stop at the corner.

He's not smiling either. *Terrific. He's going to ask me something embarrassing, isn't he?* Like where I get the inspiration for sex scenes, that sort of thing. I should've known I got off too easy on our first date. It's inevitable. Everybody wants to know where a romance writer gets her inspiration.

It's not the most terrible question in the world, but it always comes with a heavy dose of innuendo. And it seems that nine out of ten people who ask aren't satisfied when I tell them the inspiration comes from my imagination, not real life.

The alternative would be to describe my recent porn viewing, and I can't imagine that would go over well.

Then, he nudges me with a grin. "Did your grandmother ask about me when you had lunch with her?"

I can't help but burst out laughing, the kind of laughter that makes me stop in my tracks until the worst of it passes. I find him chuckling when I'm finished.

"I guess that answers my question." He laughs with me.

"Let's just say, she wasn't unhappy that I was having lunch with you," I confess. "I guess she wouldn't be a concerned grandmother if she wasn't at least a little curious."

"I had a feeling. After enough patients rotate their way through the ER, a person can spot that sort of curiosity a mile away. You know, mothers who wonder if I'm single, sisters who wonder if I have a twin brother."

"I hope you weren't offended."

"Not at all!" he insists with his trademark good-natured attitude. "Life's too short. I just thought it was funny, and I almost felt sorry for what I figured you were going to go through."

"She means well, and she only wants the best for me."

"Then, she and I have something in common."

I can't help but smile in a dorky, goofy kind of way. What can I say? He brings it out in me. "With my parents both being gone, she's the only family I have."

Yikes. Talk about a mood killer.

His face doesn't fall; it practically crashes. "Oh, Kitty. I'm sorry. I had no idea."

He looks so genuinely heartsick that I instantly feel sorry for saying it.

"I didn't mean to make you feel bad!"

"I didn't think you did. I never thought to ask. Then again, I guess we didn't really talk much about family over lunch."

"No, we didn't." I didn't want to seem like I was digging for information. *Or like, you know, that I was writing a book where the hero was a hunky doctor and I needed to get as much character background as I could manage.*

"You're an only child?"

I nod. "How about you?"

"I have a sister who lives in Atlanta. Her husband works there. They have two boys—twins, five years old. I wish I could get down there more to spend time with them."

"I bet you're a fun uncle."

He lifts an eyebrow. "What makes you say that?"

"Look at how playful you are with the dogs. And there's a sense of … I don't know." I tap my chin, squinting my eyes as I look up at him. "You have this fun energy to you. Like nothing really gets you down or stressed out. Of course, I could be completely wrong."

"I think you're pretty insightful. Does that come from being a writer? You have to observe people and imagine what their lives are like?"

"I've never thought about it that way, but I

guess you're right."

We turn the corner, coming to the dog park at Madison Square. With it being such a nice day, at least a dozen pooches are already running around like crazy and sniffing each other's butts and basically acting like the animals they are. Jake lets his dogs off their leashes, and we watch as they meet up with their friends.

I can tell my comment made him think, and a moment later, he explains why he got so thoughtful, "I wasn't always this way. You know, like you said. Easygoing. Playful, which is a word I would never have thought to use for myself."

"I hope you don't take it as an insult."

"Not even close!" He touches my shoulder, sending a shiver down my spine. "In fact, it's nice to hear. I've tried really hard to adapt to a better lifestyle, I guess you could say."

"Is it prying for me to ask, why? I mean, what brought that on?" *And please, can you keep touching me?* Of course, I would never ask that, but the impulse is there.

"I had a little bit of a scare a few years ago." He taps his chest. "I thought I was dying."

"My gosh, what happened?"

"It was a panic attack, though it felt like a heart attack to me. It's one thing to know in here that you're not having a heart attack." He taps his temple. "It's another thing to actually feel something happening to yourself, you know? I thought I was dying. I thought I was literally experiencing my last moments. That's not the sort of thing you forget."

"I am so sorry."

"I'm not. Don't get me wrong," he adds with a wry chuckle. "It sucked. But it gave me perspective, and it forced me to make changes to my life. It all starts up here." Once again, he taps his head.

Then, he claps his hands hard. "Remus, stop that!"

I turn in time to see Remus following a cocker spaniel around, insisting on sniffing her when she's clearly not into it. At the sound of Jake's voice, he gives up and sulks away.

"So, you decided to change things up?" I ask.

"Yeah, I did. When I stepped back and took a look at my life, I realized all I did was work. Mind you, I was coming off my residency, which isn't exactly a walk in the park. No pun intended," he adds, looking around us.

"What did you do?"

"I started taking care of myself. I work out a lot more than I used to, and make sure I keep to the routine. Otherwise, I try to have fun whenever I can. Even at work, which I think sometimes rubs certain people the wrong way. Like I'm not being professional enough, which couldn't be further from the truth. I take my patients very seriously, but I also believe that laughter and a positive attitude are just as helpful in healing, if not more so."

"Of course, they totally are."

He looks around the park, hands on his slim hips. "Three years ago, I would never have stood here, watching dogs play in the park. I was too busy. Life was too rigid. I hate to think of everything I missed out on."

"But just think of everything you've accomplished," I counter. "You came through all that difficult stuff, and now, you can enjoy your life a little more. That's a victory—at least, it seems that way to me."

His smile is genuine, and the hand he touches to my lower back is firm but gentle. "Thank you for that. Not everybody gets it the way you do."

"Those sourpusses at work, you mean?"

He snickers. "Yes, and other people. My ex, for one."

I should've known. Eventually, the ex always comes into the conversation.

"She's a surgeon in the same hospital," he explains. "Now that I'm down in the ER, we don't see a lot of each other there. Talk about good luck."

Terrific. How do I navigate this?

"Has it been a long time since you two broke up?"

"Oh, yeah. For almost a year. Trust me, I dodged a bullet with that one." There's bitterness in his voice, even in the way he sets his jaw. "See, I trained to be a surgeon too. She had our entire career trajectory planned out." I chuckle. "I'm serious," he adds.

"Sorry, I didn't mean to laugh at you."

He shrugs. "Anyway, when I told her I wanted to back away from surgery because the stress was getting to be too much for me, she flipped. Called me just about every name in the book, made sure I knew how disappointed she was in me. Blah, blah, blah." He touches his thumb to the tips of his other fingers, mimicking a mouth opening and closing.

I put a hand on his shoulder. "I'm sorry that happened. That she couldn't be more supportive." *Darn it, would he mind if I squeezed a little bit? I just have to know how firm this muscle is …*

He looks down at me and smiles. "It's for the best. Look who I'm out with right now. This wouldn't have happened if I were still with her—and I can imagine how stressed and miserable my life would be too."

The look in his eyes changes, and all of a sudden, I know what's about to happen. And there's no way in the world I'm about to do anything to stop him as he leans down, catching my chin between his thumb and forefinger, his mouth parting to let a sigh escape as his eyes dart down to my lips.

Just the slightest upward strain on my part as I try to meet his lips with mine is the green light he's been waiting for, and he kisses me right there in front of everyone. Including the dogs. I'm still holding on to his shoulder, and now, I give myself permission to take an exploratory squeeze while his tongue glides over my lips. Dear Lord, he's exquisite, making me wish we were someplace a little more private.

Especially when he jumps in surprise, looking down at his leg to find a terrier humping like mad. I can't help but laugh, though I at least cover my mouth with my hand while the dog's owner runs over and apologizes frantically.

"Just my animal magnetism." Jake shrugs with a sheepish grin.

"Will you come to my grandmother's birthday party with me?" I blurt out. Right, because this is the perfect time for me to ask such an important question.

Timing has never been my strong suit.

Chapter Eleven

"WHAT DID HE say?" Hayley asks.

"He said he would love to. Like, he didn't even hesitate. He jumped right in and said he would love to come with me."

"That's amazing! And terrible at the same time."

"Oh, you mean because my grandmother is going to make a big deal about it and embarrass me until I wish I were dead?"

"Yes, that's roughly what I had in mind." She sounds sympathetic at least, though there's definitely an edge of laughter in her voice.

"She'd be even worse if I didn't manage to get him on the hook for it, so I guess I have to take my victories where I can get them." I sigh, looking out over the edge of the roof, toward the park. "If he makes it through this, he might be a keeper."

"He sounds like a keeper already from what you've told me." Then, she snorts. "Except for the ex-girlfriend. There's always a stupid ex-girlfriend in the mix, isn't there?"

"I wouldn't expect somebody like him to have never dated," I point out.

"You know what I mean. You've dated before, too, but you don't parade your exes around. Not in front of somebody you only just started dating casually anyway."

"That's true. Though in the context of the story he was telling me, it made sense for him to bring her up. She didn't agree with the direction his life was going in, but he had to make a decision. He chose to take care of himself. I admire him for that; I really do."

"Jake and Kitty, sitting in a tree ..."

"Hush."

"F-U-C-K-I-N-G ..."

"Grow up." I laugh. Really, she could say just about anything to me at this point, and it wouldn't matter. I'm on cloud nine.

Because here's the thing: as much as I'm not looking forward to my grandmother embarrassing me, which I know she will, I'm very much looking forward to walking into a swanky birthday gala with an impossibly gorgeous, hunky doctor on my arm. Who wouldn't?

And it's a relief, too, that Jake didn't look at me like I'd suddenly sprouted a second head when I asked. That was what I'd expected him to do, but I should know better by now than to predict his reactions. He's a very unpredictable sort of person.

Maybe I need more of that in my life. Maybe that's part of the reason I'm so attracted to him. It makes me feel better to think this way since, otherwise, I'd have to admit I'm just in need of a good lay.

Once I get off the phone with Hayley, I get back to work. The dog park situation is just too funny to not include in a book, though I do what I can to change some of the details. My character's dogs are not huskies but golden retrievers.

What can I say? I'm not the most original person in the world, and I just sprained my ankle last weekend, thanks to a certain golden retriever. Plus, I need an energetic breed of dog, and that was the first one that came to mind.

"I should've known I'd find you up here on a day like this."

Yes, only the presence of my neighbor could dampen my spirits. Maybe not dampen my spirits exactly, but he is sort of the fly in the ointment. I only just got back to work, and now, he's joining me.

"Who could stand to be inside on a day like this?" I ask as he pulls his chair out from its customary spot under the ledge.

"Well, I obviously agree with you." He takes a seat near me, eyeing my laptop with interest. "Working on the next best seller?"

"Why do you make it sound like that's a bad thing?"

"Ouch! Take it easy. Things not going well with your hot doctor?"

Who could blame me for feeling a little bit smug

right now?

"I'll have you know, Mr. Smarty-Pants, that he just agreed to come with me to my grandmother's seventy-fifth birthday party in a couple of weeks. So, there."

He frowns. "He's coming with you to a family party?"

"Can you not sound so snide?"

"Answer my question."

"There's nothing to answer. I already told you. Yes, he's coming with me, though I think you have the wrong idea about the sort of party this is. It's not like renting out the back room of a restaurant and filling it with balloons and a collage of pictures from my grandmother's life. If anything, it might be less stressful if that were the sort of party we were going to. Grandmother is …"

"The fact that you call her *Grandmother* alone tells me a lot." Matt snickers.

"Well, she is a lot. She can be a bit much sometimes, but she's the only family I have."

"Is she rich?"

Though I know it shouldn't, his question makes me bristle, like I have something to defend. "Actually, yes, she is quite wealthy. She lives in a brownstone over on Park Avenue, and her idea of casual clothing is a silk Chanel jumpsuit. Vintage."

"I'm not quite sure what that means, but I think I can pick it up through context." He blows a low whistle through pursed lips. "And you're bringing this guy you barely know to the party?"

"She asked me to. Or rather ordered me to. I'm pretty sure I'd be turned away at the door if I showed up without him."

His eyebrows shoot up, his mouth falling open, and I immediately wish I hadn't said it. "So, you told her about him already? Bragging to Grandmother about the doctor you scored?"

"No, you idiot. She ran into us when we were having lunch outside, and that was when she saw him. Trust me, I would never have thought of it myself."

"What does he think about being part of your next book?"

Damn him. I have to look away since I don't want him to see the guilt in my eyes. "He doesn't know about that."

"Of course he doesn't," he says with a huff.

"Why should he? For Pete's sake, I've seen him twice since that day in the ER, and he's coming to a birthday party with me. It's not like we've made any promises to each other. It's not like we're even dating really."

He eyes my laptop. "How do you have the two of them meeting? Your characters, I mean."

"You'll read it in the book," I retort, tossing my hair over one shoulder.

"Let me guess. The girl hurts herself and ends up in the ER, and the doctor who treats her just happens to be the hero she's been waiting for her entire life. He just about knocks her over with his sheer sexuality, but what really gets her is how gentle and tender he is. Right?"

"Gee, you missed your calling. You should be the one who's writing."

"Tell me I'm wrong."

"You are wrong."

"How so? Don't tell me she meets him through online dating."

"No, but she does have a couple of dismal dates after trying to find a boyfriend online."

He laughs. "I'm sure none of that was drawn from real-life experience. I've noticed how you haven't done any bragging about the results of your profile yet."

"Mostly because there hasn't been anything worth bragging about." Besides, I'm not like him. I don't need to celebrate my conquests the way he does. Also, there's the fact that I haven't had any conquests lately.

"So, come on. How do they meet?"

I hate him so much right now. "Her grandmother falls and calls her for help. She takes her grandmother to the emergency room, and he is the doctor who treats her."

"So original."

"There's nothing new under the sun. Haven't you ever heard that saying?" When he laughs, I insist, "I mixed things up!"

"Yes, you just happened to include your grandmother, who is currently at the forefront of your mind because she's having a birthday party …"

"How the heck do you think writing happens, genius? This is how it's done, especially when my editor keeps telling me I need to get out and live a little. It seemed like as good a reason as any to have the two of them meet up."

"And let me guess. Does the grandmother have a birthday party, and she invites the doctor because he was so nice to her at the hospital?"

I hate him twice as much as I did just thirty seconds ago. "Now that you mention it, that's a very good way to get him at that party. Grandmother tries to hook the two of them up. They both see it for what it is and walk into it, thinking this is all funny and awkward and goofy, but they end up developing an interest in each other, which explodes in a frenzy of animal passion—"

He waves his hand, shaking his head. "Spare me, please. I don't need the sordid details."

"To be fair, there aren't any sordid details yet. But there will be."

"In the book? Or in real life?"

I meet his gaze fully, unblinking. "Maybe both. Would that be such a problem?"

"Well, I'm sure that's where his mind is going."

I roll my eyes with a sigh. "You can't possibly know that. You don't even know him."

"Neither do you."

"But I'm getting to know him."

"And I know guys. I happen to be one myself."

"No kidding!" I roll my eyes again. "I don't need a lecture on the way men's minds work. I'm not some blushing virgin even if I give the impression of one."

"I'm just saying, being a writer doesn't make you a genius when it comes to the way people think. Their motivations, you know what I mean. And I'm telling you, there's a reason why he accepted your invitation."

"Because he's a nice guy who likes me? God forbid."

"Mark my words. He's trying to get into your pants."

"You're so mean."

"I didn't know it was mean to warn a girl when another guy is trying to get her in bed. Not exactly a bad thing."

"Then, why do you make it sound like it's such a bad thing? Like there's something I need to be worried about or wary of."

He shrugs, rubbing the back of his neck and looking away from me. "I'm just saying, there are a lot of guys out there who would be willing to lead a girl in one direction, make her think they really like her, when really they just want to sleep with her. They'll do just about anything to get what they want. And when they're finished?" He shrugs.

"Speaking from experience, are we?"

That doesn't get the reaction I expected. Rather

than firing off a little quip or smirking or generally being a jerk, he shrugs again. "Yeah, I am. Why not be honest? You already think I'm a lowlife slug."

"Okay, hang on a second. I don't know that I would go that far—"

"I know you don't think I have much respect for women. There. Is that better?"

Well, I can't argue with that, so I don't bother trying.

And there's that smirk I expected, a smirk that says he knows he was right. "Like I said, I know how men think. And I don't want you … being disappointed."

Is that it? Is he only trying to help me? When I consider this, it makes me feel bad for giving him such a hard time.

I clear my throat, shifting a little in my chair because, darn it, this makes me uncomfortable. "I know what I'm in this for," I insist. "I'm not trying to catch feelings this time around. This is supposed to be fun—and for work too. I have to take this seriously."

Rather than backing off, he turns to me with a different sort of look in his eye. There's a hardness there now. "Right, and that's the other thing I have a problem with."

"No offense, but did I ask you if you had a problem with anything? Furthermore—and still no offense—does it matter? This is my life, not yours."

"I'm not allowed to tell you when I think you're

doing the wrong thing?"

I should say no, he's not allowed.

No, I should tell him it doesn't matter either way whether he thinks I'm doing the right or the wrong thing. I don't know who gave him permission to pass judgment on my life, but it sure as heck wasn't me. *Where does he get off?* The man's ego never ceases to amaze me.

"I don't remember asking for your opinion," I retort.

"I know you know it's not cool to conveniently forget to tell him he's part of a book you're writing. I know you know that."

"And yet you feel the need to say it out loud anyway," I mutter, looking up at the sky.

"That's why you can't look at me right now."

I slowly lower my head, meeting him straight-on. "Better? Trust me, that's not the reason I didn't want to look at you."

He lets this go since he's too busy attacking me. "I mean, it would be one thing if you were just casually dating and having fun. But you're taking him to a family party. That's the sort of thing that gives a person ideas. It might make them think they're more important to you than they are. I think it's only right for you to come clean."

I wish I could argue with him. I really, truly do. But I know he's right. I'm doing the same thing Blake did to me.

"I'll take your advice into consideration, okay?"

"That's a lame thing to say."

"What, you're going to criticize how I talk now too?" I barely have time to shut my laptop before springing up from my chair. "I didn't come up here to be criticized by somebody who … who …"

He holds up a hand, snickering. "Don't worry. I get the general idea. Save your words for the book you're writing."

"You'd better be careful," I warn as I fold up my chair, slamming it shut before jamming it beneath the ledge running around the edge of the roof. "You might end up in one of my books, and it won't be pretty."

"If that's the worst you can do to me, I think I'll be just fine."

Damn him for laughing as I storm away. Damn him in general.

Chapter Twelve

I DON'T THINK I've ever dreaded anything more than I'm dreading this party. Which is saying something because I have dreaded a great many things in my life.

I mean, the thought of writing a more erotic, on-trend sort of romance just about ended me. I even considered throwing in the towel during some of my darker moments.

But this? This is on a whole other level.

As I climb from the car Grandmother sent for me, it doesn't help that both my own experience with Blake and Matt's warning keeps running through my brain, and I don't know if he will consider that a sign of something serious.

I haven't seen Jake since our afternoon at the park—his work schedule has been crazy busy—and with each passing day, the question of whether or not he thinks this is more than it is has gotten bigger, heavier.

By the time I step onto the sidewalk in front of Grandmother's brownstone, there's a boulder sitting on my chest. I nod to an older couple walking arm in arm just before they turn to climb the stairs, wondering if they can tell how nervous I am.

At least there's one thing I know will go well tonight. I'm wearing Chanel, one of Grandmother's favorite brands. Not my cup of tea in general—don't get me wrong; I appreciate a well-made dress, but my style tends to be a little younger. The black cocktail dress is one of a few she bought for me after my college graduation, when she was sure I'd rise to the top of the literary world and need suitable clothes for all the fancy parties I'd attend.

What would she think if she knew what I was writing now? Honestly, she'd probably love it.

Now is most definitely not the time to be thinking about that. I don't need to stress myself out even more.

His timing is impeccable. Just as I turn around to look in the other direction, wondering if maybe Jake forgot about our meeting up at eight in front of the house, I catch sight of a man at least a head taller than everyone around him, strolling down the avenue.

Hot. Diggity. Dog. He's wearing a tuxedo that looks like it was made just for him—heck, it probably was since I doubt he could grab anything off the rack with a body like that. He walks with calm, grace, elegance. He doesn't even register the fact that just about everybody who passes by stops to take a second look at him.

His hair, normally wild and wavy, is slicked back in a neat, short ponytail. His tanned face is freshly shaven. There's a bow tie at his throat, which I want nothing more than to remove with my teeth. Only the slight smirk playing over his lips when he finds me gaping at him in flat-out surprise gives away the goofball underneath the polished surface.

"Wow," I breathe when he reaches me. "You look like James Bond right now."

"Oh?" His eyes light up before he falls into a pose, one hand in his pocket, the other at his slightly upturned chin. He lowers his brow. "Becker. Jake Becker."

"Stop it." I giggle. "Before somebody crashes their car from staring at you." Really, I'm surprised there hasn't been a massive pileup as it is.

"Me? Look at you!" He lets out a low whistle, nodding in appreciation. "You're stunning."

I can't help but touch a self-conscious hand to my hair, arranged in a twist at the back of my head. I usually like to keep it down, but I don't feel like seeing my grandmother's disappointed stares all night. "You really think so?"

"I think nobody will be able to take their eyes off you tonight." He juts out his elbow. "Shall we?"

Oh, yes, we shall.

I take his arm—*the muscles, oh my gosh, what I wouldn't give to have him out of this tux*—and walk with him up the wide staircase.

"Miss Kathryn!" Peter's all decked out, too, in a coat with tails and everything. He nods his head in greeting to Jake.

"Peter, this is Dr. Jake Becker," I murmur with more than a little pride. Okay, so maybe I'm a little jazzed about being at the party with a doctor who could easily moonlight as a model. Or a secret agent. "Peter's been with my grandmother for as long as I can remember, and sometimes, I like him a lot more than I like her."

This gets a laugh from him, which I sense isn't strictly the way he's supposed to behave during a fancy function like this. "You'll find her in the library," he says before turning to the couple arriving behind us.

"Wow. This is impressive," Jake whispers, taking it all in.

I've been here a hundred times, and even I'm more than a little amazed. I'm pretty sure she must've bought out the entirety of the city's floral shops in preparation for this. The sweeping staircase along one wall has been festooned with lush roses, hydrangea, peonies—all of them in shades of cream and light pink. The chandeliers cast rainbows of light along the walls and ceiling as the dangling bits of crystal move and sway.

A server walks past with a silver tray covered in champagne flutes.

"Thank you," I murmur, taking one.

Jake's still a little shell-shocked, so I take one for

him as well.

"You okay?" I whisper with a smile, handing him a flute.

"I didn't expect this," he admits. "I mean, I figured … but this …"

"If it's too much, we can go." It's not like I was looking forward to it for any personal reasons. I'm here out of duty. "We can show our faces, mingle a little, and then cut out."

"Of course we can't do that," he scolds, though he's gentle about it. Probably surprised that I'd suggest it. "She's your grandmother, and she wants you to be here. Plenty of people don't make it to seventy-five."

He's right, and I guess he'd know all about that.

"I don't want you to feel obligated, is all. You don't owe me anything." *Damn that Matt for getting in my head. I could kill him.*

Jake only shoots me a puzzled look. "Why would I? You were nice enough to ask me. Come on. Let's see how the other half lives." There's that glimmer in his eye again, or maybe it's the light from the chandeliers. Or maybe some fancy lady's diamond earrings are sparkling somewhere nearby.

I have a feeling this is going to be an interesting night.

"Darling!" Grandmother extends both arms, and I have to wonder how she can manage to lift them with heavy diamond cuffs on each wrist. "I was afraid you wouldn't make it."

"How could I miss this?" I ask with a smile. *Especially since you made it clear you'd never forgive me if I didn't come.* Not that she said those exact words, mind you, but some things don't need to be said.

As soon as her gaze hits Jake, I might as well not be in the room. "Dr. Becker, I'm thrilled you found time in your busy schedule to be here," she purrs, shaking his hand.

Now that she's not wearing those huge sunglasses, I can see the way her eyes move over him. Like she's already imagining what our children will look like.

Or like she's got ideas about having him for herself. I don't know whether that thought should make me laugh or gag a little. I settle on a sip of champagne to hide my grin.

"I'm honored you included me on your guest list," Jake assures her. "This is a beautiful home and such a special occasion."

He's perfect. He's freaking perfect. So smooth. Grandmother's practically swooning.

"By all means, enjoy yourselves." She smiles, as there's another group of people waiting to wish her a happy birthday.

She grabs my arm just as I'm turning away. "If you don't lock him down, you're out of the will," she hisses in my ear.

I wish I thought she was kidding.

"We're the youngest people here," Jake observes in a soft voice as we walk from room to room.

There are still flowers everywhere along with lit candles, which provide soft, romantic light. Though I'm not fooled. The soft lighting makes my grandmother look younger, so she prefers it.

"By decades," I whisper, nodding to one of my grandmother's friends who I vaguely recognize.

Of course, she takes this as an invitation to descend upon us.

Shoot. What's her name again?

"Kathryn, dear, you look beautiful, as always." Only it's not me she's interested in. I'm starting to feel like I might as well be a piece of furniture. She turns to Jake, tipping her head back to beam up at him. "Whitney Wilson," she coos, extending a hand.

Right. One of my grandmother's oldest frenemies. They've been throwing thinly veiled insults at each other since finishing school, though I have no doubt they'd both kill for the other if it came to that.

"Jake Becker." He smiles.

"Dr. Becker, from what I've heard," she adds, teasing. "Don't downplay your accomplishments. Cecile told me all about you and Kathryn, and I couldn't be happier."

"Um, Mrs. Wilson?" I whisper, tugging the sleeve of her silk jacket.

But Jake handles it well. "I'm just lucky she thinks I'm worth spending time with," he sighs with a shrug.

"Goodness," Whitney practically moans, eyes

roaming over his body.

"We were just on our way to get something to eat."

Okay, so maybe I could've said that a bit more quietly, but the woman sounded like she was about to orgasm. I take his elbow and steer him away, toward the dining room where the clinking of plates tells me there's a light meal laid out.

"I am so sorry," I hiss in horror once we're out of earshot. "That was uncalled for."

"It's okay." He chuckles. "She was just being nice."

Yeah, nice.

"And I didn't tell my grandmother we're together or anything like that," I add in a tight whisper. "That's the truth."

"That's also how grandmothers are. Mothers, too, and fathers." He stops me before we reach the dining room, taking my arms in his hands. "Hey. It's okay. I knew what I was getting into when I agreed to come here tonight. I'm not a babe in the woods. You don't have to protect me."

He's right. I can breathe a little easier, knowing he's not half as mortified as I am.

"I just don't want you thinking I brought you here to, you know, trap you or something like that."

"Believe me, I don't think anything like that. Although"—he raises an eyebrow along with one corner of his mouth—"if you wanted to trap me, I wouldn't fight too hard to get away."

I wish my heart wouldn't pound quite so hard. I can hardly hear him over the sound of it. "I'll have to dig the net out from the back of my closet. And the ropes."

"Oh? That sort of talk will only earn you an early exit, young lady."

That's bad enough. It's when he catches his bottom lip under his teeth that I have to forcefully will myself not to wrap my arms and legs around him and climb him like a tree.

"Kathryn! We're dying to meet your doctor!" another of Grandmother's friends calls out from the dining room. "Come, let's get a look at you two together!"

"What was that about an early exit?" I mutter out of the corner of my mouth, which makes him laugh.

He takes my hand. "Come on. Let's give them what they want."

Chapter Thirteen

"ARE YOU STILL writing your little books, Kathryn?"

Doggone it. I shouldn't have drained that third champagne. It's making my brain move way too slowly, and now that people have stopped asking about Jake and started asking about my work, I need every ounce of mental acuity I can manage.

"I am." I smile since it's not worth addressing the whole *little books* jab.

These people are so good at wrapping an insult in what sounds like kindness. I'm pretty sure passive-aggressive backbiting is a graduate-level course they're all required to take before graduating high school.

Please leave it there. Please leave it there. Don't ask for details—

"And what's your next book about?" The question comes from the woman of the hour herself, who saw fit to join the little group that somehow magically gathered around me when yet another of her friends asked about my books in a way that made it clear she thought they were a joke.

I shoot my grandmother what can only be described as a withering look before smiling. She knows darn well since she already asked me that question while we were having lunch together. "It's about a girl who meets a doctor actually."

Here's the thing: if I lied, she would've called me out on it because that's how she rolls. And lying would have only made it look like I had something to hide.

I steal a glance up at Jake, whose face is an unreadable mask. What does he think about this? This is not the way I intended to tell him.

There I was, thinking tonight was perfect. Planning to ask him back to my place even. Not usually the move I make on the third date, but this is not an average situation. Not for me anyway.

I mean, he's wearing a tuxedo. My heart can barely take it.

Now? I'll be lucky if he stays the entire evening.

"No, really?" Grandmother looks up at Jake, all innocent, pretending this is news to her. The little snake. "I wonder if he bears a resemblance to you, Dr. Becker."

"The book is only partly written. I mean, very vague outlines. Nothing concrete." I wish I could disappear. Just vanish into thin air.

"I expect it to be light and fun and enjoyable, the way your other books have been." That's Mrs. Wilson, who managed to slide into the group when I wasn't looking. She's been watching Jake all night and not bothering to pretend otherwise.

I wonder if I'll ever get to the point in my life where I don't give a damn what anybody thinks about my behavior. Though having millions of dollars to her name probably gives her that extra shot of confidence.

"I didn't know you read my work," I offer with a laugh I certainly don't feel. *Shoot, shoot, shoot.* My skin's turning all kinds of hot, and my palms are suddenly sweaty. *Why did Maggie insist on publishing the more graphic work under my actual name?*

"To be fair, I've only read your first two books," she explains with a tiny grimace. "But I thought they were charming. Delightful."

"Will your next book be as charming and delightful?" Jake asks.

So, he remembers how to speak. I don't know if that's a good thing or a bad thing, to be honest. His face is still unreadable.

"It depends on what my editor asks for." I shrug. *Am I sweating? I must be sweating.* I'm probably dripping sweat onto the floor. *Why are so many people looking at me?* There's a reason I spend most of my life behind a keyboard. I can't deal with this.

Whitney puts a hand on Jake's arm. "Come now. I'm sure that with a subject like this, you can't help but write something your readers will want to devour."

Is it my imagination, or are her fingers pressing into his arm just a little harder than they need to?

"The book isn't about him specifically," I rush to clarify.

He hates me; he has to hate me after this. How could I ever look at him again? I should've known this was all too good to be true.

"Then, who is it about?" Grandmother asks.

Seriously? Is she trying to make me squirm? Because she's doing a pretty good job of it.

"It's about a character who exists up here." I tap a finger to my temple. "The way all of my books are."

Good thing my name isn't Pinocchio because my nose would've impaled the three-tier showpiece of a birthday cake in the center of the dining room table by now.

"Come now. We all know writers draw inspiration from the people they know in real life," Whitney points out.

"That's very true, but I wouldn't want anyone to recognize themselves in one of my books."

Note to self: make sure to write about a cougar with millions who has a hard time keeping her hands to herself. Name her Whitney.

"Well, with all this magnificent raw material to write about, I can't imagine how you could pass up the opportunity."

It is definitely not my imagination. Whitney very blatantly squeezes Jake's arm again. Now that she's had a few drinks, she's even less discreet.

Jake clears his throat. "I could use a glass of

water," he murmurs, even going so far as to slide a finger under the collar of his shirt like it's choking him. "It's a little crowded in here."

"I'll show you to the kitchen," I offer since there isn't anyone walking around with water on trays. Only champagne, hors d'oeuvres, that sort of thing.

"One of the staff can fetch water for him," Grandmother reminds me.

"It's all right. Let them do their jobs. I think I can handle finding the sink." I then practically drag Jake behind me, hardly even looking where I'm going and just barely avoiding knocking a server into the table and thus the cake.

This is a nightmare. This is exactly the sort of thing I was afraid would happen. If there could possibly be a worse time for Jake to learn about the subject of my book, I don't know when it could be.

The butler's pantry is just off the kitchen, and I duck in there with Jake close behind me. It's dark and cool in here, most of the commotion taking place in the kitchen. I have to lean against the countertop and catch my breath.

"I didn't really need water," Jake murmurs, standing against the counter opposite mine.

"I didn't think you did. I'm so sorry that happened."

"Sorry that you conveniently forgot to tell me you were writing about a doctor? Or sorry that it came out when it did, the way it did? Because clearly, you were planning on telling me very soon.

Right?" There's something in his voice that tells me how I need to answer this question. It's not really a question at all but rather a statement I'd better agree with or else.

"Of course I was going to tell you. But I wasn't kidding; I haven't written that much. Much less than I should have by now, to tell you the truth."

"Why? Because I haven't provided enough inspiration yet?" he whispers.

"It's not like that," I insist, also keeping my voice low. "I swear. And I make it a point to change details, so it's not like anybody could identify you as being the subject."

"That's not what I care about. Here I was, thinking you wanted to spend time with me because of me, not because of some book you were writing."

"That's not how it is!" I let my head fall back, staring up at the ceiling. "What a mess. This is all wrong. Of course I want to spend time with you. I like you so much. And to be fair, I already knew the hero of my next book would be a doctor when I met you. It's not like I'm that much of an opportunist."

"No, but you just so happened to meet me, and you just so happened to call me …"

It's so dark, I can hardly see his face when I go from staring at the ceiling to looking at him. I wish I could tell how he looks since that would give me one more clue as to how he's feeling about this.

"I called you because … I mean, okay, straight talk. Look at you. You're gorgeous; you had a personality that put me at ease in the ER. Who wouldn't call you if given the opportunity?"

Then, I can't help but giggle softly. "I know Mrs. Wilson would. You'll probably see her in the ER in the coming days."

He turns his face away, snorting. "That's a totally different story," he sighs.

Okay, so he's not in a joking mood.

"I don't want you to think I'm using you. That's the last thing I want to do. I admit, sometimes, work and personal life get mixed up a little, but I promise that anything I write will be absolutely glowing. Any negative characteristics of my hero would have nothing to do with you. I know how to fictionalize real-life events. Trust me, I've had plenty of experience with that."

"Oh?" He turns to me. "How much experience?"

Could I be imagining this? Does he sound playful again?

"None of your business," I venture with a smirk. "You know what I mean."

"I do. It threw me a little, is all."

"You can demand I not write about a doctor, if you want. I'm serious. That's completely up to you. I'm still early enough in the process that I can change the character to a lawyer or a dentist or a doorman, for heaven's sake. Whatever you want."

He's quiet for so long, dread takes root in my heart.

"Or," I add in a whisper when I can't stand the

silence another moment, "you can tell me to get lost and refuse to see me again. I'd totally understand."

"What?" he asks. "You think I don't want to see you anymore?"

"Uh, well, I mean …"

He takes a step closer and then another until we're standing toe to toe. "That's not what I was thinking at all," he whispers an instant before his fingertips skim my forearm.

My breath catches, but I manage to ask, "What were you thinking?"

"I was thinking …" He leans down, closer and closer, until his breath tickles my neck when he murmurs in my ear, "I need to up my game if you're writing about me for your next book."

I can barely formulate a thought before his hands find my waist. In one quick motion, he lifts me onto the counter.

"Jake!" I gasp, surprised and almost painfully aroused at this sudden turn of events. "What are you doing?"

"What I've been wanting to do since the second I set eyes on you tonight." He takes my face in both hands, and in the dim light coming in from the door between the kitchen and pantry, I can see his eyes boring into mine. "Unless you don't want me to," he adds in a throaty growl that curls my toes.

"I want you to," I admit before his kiss sweeps me away, and there's nothing to be done but wind my arms around his neck and hold on tight.

"We're going to get in trouble," I whisper as he trails kisses down my throat.

He nudges my dress up just a little, so I can part my legs enough for him to step between them. Oh dear Lord, the feeling of him between my thighs is heaven.

He groans when I wrap my legs around his thighs, pulling him closer. "If you keep doing things like that, yeah, we are," he agrees before capturing my mouth again.

I can't help it. My hands slide underneath his jacket like they have a mind of their own and travel the many hills and planes of his body. His broad back, tapering down to his waist. Then, between us to explore his rippling abs, his bulging chest. His heart's hammering in there, just like mine is.

"Kitty ..." he groans, teeth clenched, his breath coming fast and hot against my neck. "I want you."

A shudder runs through me when those three simple words hit home. I part my lips, ready to tell him how desperately I want him, too, when light suddenly floods into the room.

I gasp, clutching him as he lifts his head to look toward the open door with me.

"Oh, don't let me stop you," Grandmother says, waving a hand. "I was going to announce we're about to cut the cake, but that's not important. Go on ahead. Take your time. We'll wait for you."

"Oh my God," I sigh, closing my eyes. *This can't be happening.*

"Be sure to fix your lipstick before you come out, dear," she continues and then, "You, too, Doctor."

When the door swings shut, Jake just about collapses against me in helpless laughter.

Thank God he has a good sense of humor.

Chapter Fourteen

"SHOULD WE REALLY be doing this in here?" Nikki asked in a whisper, almost laughing at how unbelievable the situation was. "Won't you get into trouble?"

Jeff gripped her hips, pulling her closer to the edge of the counter. "I thought you came in here for an exam," he growled, his already-dark eyes darkening further as they moved over her body.

"Is this the way you treat all your female patients, Doctor?"

"Only the ones who do to me what you do."

There was no chance to offer anything more before he cut her off with a deep, searching kiss, his tongue plunging in and out of her mouth the way she wished he would plunge in and out of other places. Places that now hummed and tingled, thanks to the attention his hands were paying to her jean-clad thighs, to that little strip of bare skin at the top of her waistband.

She knew she should be a good girl and gently but firmly push him away. She should shake a finger at him and accuse him of being a very bad boy for trying to do this at work, in one of his exam rooms.

She should.

But for some reason, she chose instead to slide her hands under his white lab coat and push it back over his shoulders, to work the buttons of his shirt so her hands could feel his warm skin, over the muscles flexing just underneath.

He closed a hand over her breast, molding it in his palm, groaning into her mouth.

"Shh!" she whispered, flushed and giddy, and he nipped at her neck in response until she had to bury her face against his shoulder and bite her lip or else risk giving them away.

Yes, this is good. Just enough like what happened in the butler's pantry but changed up enough that it fits the book's trope.

It's hard to write this without getting swept up in the memories of what really did happen. How exciting it was to walk the line between passion and danger. Not that the danger was as serious as the trouble my characters could get into if somebody were to walk in and find them screwing in an exam room in the middle of a busy workday.

But if it had been anyone else but my grandmother who stepped through that door and discovered us on the verge of whatever we were on the verge of, it could've made for a very embarrassing end to the evening. As it was, I couldn't meet her gaze for the rest of the night—not that we stayed very long after that. Once the cake was cut, the guests started drifting away one and two at a time.

I made sure we joined the exodus before Whitney Wilson could sink her claws any deeper into Jake.

For all I know, Grandmother is currently planning on throwing a shower to celebrate the arrival of her first great-grandchild.

"She wasn't really as okay with that as she seemed, was she?" Jake asked once we were outside.

"Don't let appearances fool you," I reminded him. "I'm surprised she didn't stick around to give us instructions. Not that she is a pervert or anything, but she's very … open-minded for somebody her age."

"I would like to get to know her better." He grinned.

"Something tells me the feeling is mutual," I sighed, glancing up at the house and wondering if Whitney Wilson was watching.

Considering how badly the night could've gone, things ended up not so bad after all. Aside from the fact that I came home alone since Jake made a point to warn me that he had to be in the ER early the next morning, I don't think it could've gone better.

Especially since he promised we could pick up where we'd left off whenever I wanted. As far as I was concerned at the time, that meant in the backseat of the cab. No such luck, though we did do a little smooching before he left me outside my building.

Nothing nearly as hot as what went down in the pantry, and I'm definitely craving more as my thoughts keep returning to that same point in the night.

What's happening to me? Am I turning into some sort of sex addict?

No. In fact, the opposite is true, I think.

It's been so long since I had a regular partner that every little sexy, exciting situation replays itself over and over in my head because its rareness makes it even more special.

Though the fact that Jake played a part in it has a lot to do with that, I'm guessing. Now that I've seen how naughty he's willing to be, a whole new crop of fantasies are just waiting to be explored. I wonder how many of them will make it into this book.

Frankly, a man as sexy as Jake could just stand still in one place and not say a word, and I could come up with enough filthy scenarios to fill an entire series of books.

For once, the site of my editor's name on my phone's screen doesn't fill my heart with dread. For once, I can tell her things are going well, and that's what I do as soon as I pick up the call. "The words are flowing," I chirp in lieu of a greeting.

"That's good to hear," Maggie chirps right back. "So, your first pass will make the deadline?"

"Most definitely," I announce with a lot more confidence than I feel.

Really, there's nobody stopping me from meeting my deadline, except for me. I have to push through the days when the words don't want to come—and that's the same no matter what I'm writing, no matter the tropes or anything like that.

"Excellent! So ..." The woman is practically overflowing with curiosity. I can hear it in her voice.

"You want to know who this book is about? Is that what you're trying to ask me without actually saying it out loud?"

"Wouldn't you want to know if you were in my shoes? I mean, the entire story hinges upon its hero and heroine—"

"You don't have to defend yourself," I sigh. "It just so happens, I met a doctor recently."

"Through the dating site?"

"How did you know about that?"

Silence. Then, "I might have checked in with your friend Hayley when I didn't hear from you for a day or two. I wanted to be sure you were on the way to the next book without making you feel like I was hounding you."

It's enough to make my head hurt. I rub the bridge of my nose, trying to push it back. "You don't have to do that. Please, don't do that again. She has a life and a career of her own. Okay?"

"Fine. Be more communicative then."

"Fine."

"So, was it through the site?"

"No, I did it the old-fashioned way. I ended up in the emergency room—everything is fine," I add when she gasps. "But it did lead me to him, so things could have been much worse."

"Describe."

When she starts talking in one-worded sentences, I know better than to drag my feet.

"The man's muscles have muscles," I gush. Okay, so maybe it's a little gross, talking about him this way, but I know Maggie won't leave me alone until I paint a picture. Blake Marlin, she could look up online. For all I knew, she might have met him in person before we started dating.

"A promising start."

"He oozes sensuality, but he has a playful spirit. He's never too serious, so he's always up for fun."

"Naughty fun? Sexy fun?"

"You sound so hopeful."

"Can you blame me?"

No, I guess I can't. Rather than leave her hanging, I giggle. "Yes, naughty and sexy fun. I'm not getting any further into details," I warn before she can ask any questions that have me truly cringing.

"No fair."

"You'll have to wait to read about it," I tease.

"Can you at least send me a few chapters to peruse?" It's almost cute, the way she phrases that like an actual question. Like she's not ordering me as my editor to provide a few chapters so she's clear on the direction I'm taking the book. Like we haven't worked together for years, like I don't know the way things go.

But I'm still riding high after last night and living in hope of picking up where we left off, so I'm feeling generous enough to bite back a sarcastic comment. "Of course," I assure her. "I can send you something tonight once I polish up whatever I worked on over the weekend."

"Wonderful. I can hardly wait. I guess I'll leave you to it then," she adds before ending the call in her usual abrupt way. As friendly and kissy-kissy as she tries to act, this is a business relationship after all.

I only wish she hadn't taken me out of the scene I was working on before she called. Okay, so my hero and heroine are in the examination room, and they're about to get it on with patients and other staff members walking back and forth on the other side of the door. Exciting, dangerous, and all of it makes things feel so much sexier.

Now, I know that for a fact.

Maybe Maggie was right. Maybe I needed to experience certain things for myself before writing about them.

By the time my phone buzzes again, another couple of hours have passed, and I'm editing the chapters I plan to send to Maggie. There's nothing like knowing your editor wants to read something to get those fingers moving over the keys. Granted, sometimes, the pressure ends up resulting in writer's block, but that hasn't been the case today. Thank goodness.

I'm so busy trying to finish things up that I barely take notice of the text, when my phone buzzes. Only Jake's name could yank me out of my work frenzy—even Hayley would normally have to wait for a response.

How about I make it up to you tonight?

I love a man who gets right to the point.

What do you have in mind? I ask, biting my lip.

You. Me. My place. Takeout. Maybe a movie … maybe not.

Oh boy. I have to fan myself since, all of a sudden, it feels like the temperature in the room just jumped up.

Any specific time in mind? I ask, already imagining what I'll wear. And I don't mean which jeans or top I should pick.

A situation like this calls for sexy underwear.

Seven o'clock? I have a few errands to run, and I could swing by the Chinese restaurant down the street to pick up food and bring it back.

That sounds good to me, and I tell him so. It gives me another hour to finish my work, take a special shower—the kind of shower a girl takes when she knows the night's going to go in a certain direction—and hustle over to his apartment.

Is it totally sick that I can't help thinking how pleased Maggie would be if she knew what was happening tonight? Yes, it's definitely pretty sick. I need to get her out of my head. My personal life is my own. It doesn't belong to her or to my readers.

I'm still telling myself this as I climb out of the car in front of Jake's building. It's one of those newly renovated buildings with all the amenities a young professional requires nowadays—a gym, a coffee shop in the lobby, a dry cleaner, even maid service.

Maybe I should move into a place like this. Then, I wouldn't even have to leave the building to get my caffeine fix. And I wouldn't have to deal with certain pesky neighbors.

Darn it. I need to get Matt out of my head too.

It's only a couple of minutes to seven when I knock on the door to Jake's apartment, close to the top floor. There is a skittering of paws on wood, telling me the dogs are freaking out at the idea of a visitor. I brace myself for the impending attack the second the door opens.

Only, when the door swings open, it's not a husky attack that hits me or the sight of a clean, spacious apartment.

It's the stunning young woman who opened the door. The woman standing there with one hand on her hip, looking me up and down. "Yes?"

Chapter Fifteen

IF IT WASN'T for the dogs running around behind her, I might think I had the wrong apartment. "Sorry. I'm looking for Jake?"

"He's not home right now," she informs me, still studying me like I'm some species she's never seen before.

"He … asked me to meet him here. I'm sorry, who are you?"

Her perfectly arched brows meet when she scowls. "I'm someone who's not about to let you inside until Jake shows up and tells me it's okay."

Great. What is she, a detective? Somebody who's used to interrogating people and knows how to avoid answering direct questions?

My skin crawls as this woman—tall, willowy, devastatingly beautiful—stares me down. Here I am, standing in the hallway, feeling like a total idiot, while she blocks the way into the apartment.

And where the heck is Jake?

I lick my lips, which have suddenly gone dry. "Well, he told me he'd pick up food before coming back here. I guess something must've held him up."

"I guess it did."

Darn it, that didn't work. I hoped maybe once I confirmed what Jake's plans were, she would come around and figure out that I must know him, that we must have made plans to meet up. No such luck. *Shouldn't I know better by now?*

I'm just about to ask what gives her the right to be in Jake's apartment when he's not there when the elevator doors open. I could just about faint with relief when they do, especially since Jake steps out with shopping bags in both hands.

"Hey." He grins when he sees me. A grin that dissolves when he sees who's standing on the other side of the apartment door. "Erin? What are you doing here?"

Yes, I would like to know the answer to that question too.

I turn to her with a smile, brows lifting. How quickly the tables have turned.

"I told you, I had to come back and grab some of my things. This is the first chance I've had since I got back." At least she's gracious enough to step aside, so I can enter, followed by the man whose apartment this is in the first place.

Grab some of her things?

Oh no. Tell me this isn't the ex-girlfriend. But I thought they broke up ages ago. Why would he still have her things?

"Great. You can leave your key, too, while you're at it." Jake brushes past her, heading straight for the kitchen.

It's an open layout, meaning I can see everything he does from where I stand by the front door. The fact is, the air in the apartment is so tense, I'm not sure what I should do. So, I don't do anything but stand there, waiting to be directed.

"Yeah, I'll do that," Erin mutters, pulling a ring of keys from her purse and going through them as she speaks.

"Is there anything else you need?" he asks, coming back from the kitchen and joining me. His arm slides around my waist for good measure.

I'm not dumb. I know that a big part of the reason he did that was to make sure she knows he's not withering on the vine now that she's gone. He wants to send a silent message that there's somebody new in his life.

Even so, the little thrill of victory that shoots up my spine at his touch is pretty nice. It's not my fault she is such a snooty thing.

Her gaze flits down to where his hand rests at my waist before darting back up to him. "I guess not," she mutters, slinging her purse over one shoulder and picking up a paper bag that I assume holds whatever she came to collect.

Once she's out in the hall and the door's closed, Jake leans against it. "Her timing is still impeccable," he mutters. Then, he turns to me. "I'm sorry about that. Let's just forget that happened, okay?"

"Sure." I shrug, though I can't help but feel a

little sideways after what I just witnessed.

Why did she still have a key? Did they really break up as long ago as he said? I can't stop asking myself these questions even though I know it would be better to move on and act like it didn't happen.

"Good. I brought back enough food to feed at least five people, so I hope you're hungry." He greets the dogs finally, and they both soak up his attention before practically tackling me to the floor. At least when he scolds them, they obey. Maybe they are trained after all.

I probably shouldn't ask, should I? I should pretend that little bit of awkwardness didn't happen, just like he wants me to do. It'll only make things worse if I bring it up.

Then again, I know myself. I know I won't be able to stop thinking about that glorious Amazon of a woman who just walked out of here.

"I'm sorry, but I have to ask. Was that your ex-girlfriend? The one you told me about?"

His shoulders slump a little. "Do we have to do this?"

"I'm not trying to do anything. I'm curious, especially since she treated me like an intruder when she opened the door."

"That won't happen again," he promises. "I admit, I should've been more diligent when it came to getting her key back, but she was overseas for eight months on a research project. When she came back, part of me figured it wasn't such a bad idea for somebody else to have a key in case something happened here. If I was stuck at the hospital and the dogs needed feeding or walking."

I have half a mind to remind him that there are services for situations like that. Heck, in a building like his, I wouldn't be surprised if they had somebody on staff who could take care of those little incidents should they come up.

Either he can hear my thoughts or we're of the same mind on this.

"I know those are just excuses," he admits with a sigh. "It's never an easy thing to do, cutting those last few ties. Having you here with me gave me the strength to do it, especially since I got the feeling she was being rude toward you."

He comes to me, planting a kiss on top of my head before giving me a quick hug. "I'm sorry. Now, can we forget about her for good?"

"I look forward to it." I smile.

After that, we take the food out to the coffee table before sinking into the big, overstuffed sofa. I guess he needs big furniture like this, being as large as he is.

"They are really well behaved," I observe of the dogs, who sit patiently and watch as Jake unloads one container after another from the bag.

"It's only when they get excited at being outside that they forget themselves a little," he explains with a fond look in their direction. "That's when they start aggressively sniffing the butts of other dogs, but you know that from having seen it for yourself."

"Yes, I do remember that." I also remember the terrier who humped the daylights out of his leg, but I'll spare him the memory. "I recall almost getting my arm pulled off too."

"You'll get used to that. We'll strengthen you up."

I don't know if he knows what he just said, whether it was a slip of the tongue or something deliberate. But he definitely made it sound like he expects me to be around for a while.

Of course, he won't get an argument out of me if that's the case. I want to be around. Very much.

"Jeez, were you expecting additional guests?" I ask when I finally take in the amount of food on the table. When he suggested Chinese, it's not like I was going to say no. It's probably my favorite kind of takeout. There's lo mein, fried rice, broccoli with garlic sauce, sweet and sour chicken, sautéed tofu with vegetables, an entire metal container of eggrolls.

"I wanted to make sure we had something you liked." He shrugs with a sheepish little smile. "That's all."

I can't help but lean in to kiss his scruffy cheek. "You're a sweetheart."

He smiles, leaning in like he's about to kiss me. "So are you."

Oh, yes. Food be damned. I'm about ready to let

him lay me down on the couch and—

The sound of his stomach rumbling makes us both laugh.

"Hmm. First things first," he mutters.

If he thinks I'm going to pig out, he's got another thing coming. It would be one thing if I had nothing more than a nervous stomach to deal with. I mean, there's a really good chance tonight is going to end very well—wink, wink, nudge, nudge. Anybody would be a little nervous.

On top of that, there's the memory of what happened when I went to Blake's apartment and had dinner before fooling around. I barely made it through the horrific embarrassment of burping like a longshoreman while we were making out.

Though I know now that I mishandled the situation and shouldn't have reacted the way I did.

Still, I can't think of much that's less sexy than somebody letting out an echoing belch. And after seeing what came before me in the form of Little Miss Erin with her raven hair and pouty lips and surgeon's skill, it feels more important than ever to make a good impression. I bet she never let out a belch like that during a key moment.

This is why I pick at a few different things while we watch a comedy on TV. A nice TV, wide-screen, the picture so sharp and clear that it's like we're right there with the actors. Aside from that and the elaborate game system under the TV, there really isn't much in the apartment to give away how well-off he is. He's a very humble person, and like he said, his priorities have shifted.

"Are you not hungry?" he asks, noting how little I've taken on my plate.

"No, I am, and it's all delicious." I pop a piece of chicken into my mouth like that's going to convince him. It really is good, too, perfectly crispy and not the least bit oily. *I need to get the number to this place.*

"Are you comfortable? Should I adjust the air-conditioning?" He even leans forward, like he's about to get up from the couch.

I shake my head, waving him back. "I'm fine. Thank you. Everything's great."

Instead of relaxing against the couch cushions, which I hoped my reassurance would lead him to do, he rubs his hands over his thighs. His thick, muscular thighs. Thighs my legs have been wrapped around. Oh boy, I need to snap my attention back to the current moment.

"I just want you to be comfortable. I want you to feel at home and relaxed. It's important to me."

The simplicity and earnestness in his voice touches my heart in ways I can't describe. He's so genuine, so sweet.

And so damn sexy. Maybe even sexier because he's so kind.

Which is why I lean forward to place my plate on the table before practically throwing myself at him.

"Whoa!" He laughs, sitting back as I straddle his

lap. "What brought that on?"

"You," I breathe, leaning down until our foreheads touch. "Just you."

His hands slide up my back, a smile creeping over his face. "Then, I guess I have to thank myself," he whispers before catching my mouth. His arms wrap around my back and pull me tight, practically forcing me against what's already growing in his jeans.

Forget dinner. This is much more delicious.

He holds me in place, shifting positions until I'm on my back and he's on top of me, and he kisses me for all he's worth, one hand moving up and down from my shoulder to my ankle and back again.

My skin is on fire, nerves tingling, heat spreading in my core. He wants to know why I didn't eat very much? This is why I didn't eat very much. Because this is what I really want. For once, Kitty Valentine is going to give herself what she really wants.

Buzz! Buzz!

"You've got to be kidding me," Jake mutters with a heavy sigh before pushing himself up on both arms so he can wiggle the phone out of his pocket. "Sorry about this."

"No problem." *Sure, I'm lying here underneath you with my blouse practically unbuttoned and my chest heaving and my skin flushed. No problem.*

Rather than tossing the darn thing aside, which I really wish he would do, he takes a look at the screen. He's a doctor. I guess he can't afford to disregard a random phone call. There might be an emergency someplace.

Granted, I have no idea how these things work, but I'm guessing it's possible.

"I'm sorry. I should take this. She's already texted, like, ten times. She's not going to stop."

Before I even have the chance to ask who he's talking about, he's off the couch and answering the call. The man's jeans are still tented in the front—and quite a respectable tent, I must say, the sort of tent that makes a girl wonder if she can handle everything a man is packing—but he's answering the phone.

"What?" he barks.

And all of a sudden, I know exactly who's on the other end. And exactly what drove her to text him so many times. And exactly why she felt the need to call him. Because she knew I would still be here, and she wanted to get in the way.

He goes to another room, closing the door, but I can still hear him arguing, even over the TV and the dogs, who are now nervously pacing back and forth, sensing Jake's anger.

After a few minutes of this, I decide to sit up, button my shirt, and go back to eating. Romulus sits on one side, Remus on the other, and the three of us continue watching the movie while I eat to my heart's content and occasionally give them a piece of chicken.

Why not? The mood's been ruined, so there's no sense in starving myself anymore.

Chapter Sixteen

"I SHOULD'VE KNOWN better."

"Don't say that."

"Even if it's true?"

Hayley shoots me a scowl from across the table. "So, his ex called. Granted, yes, that was a deliberate move on her part. I'm surprised she waited as long as she did."

"Yeah, and she got exactly what she wanted. He was in there, fighting with her, for almost an hour. The movie was over by the time he finished, and his food was cold."

She lowers her brow, giving me one of her stern looks. "She got what she wanted because neither of you bothered to pick up where you'd left off."

"There is such a thing as being in the moment, Hayley. And after hearing him fight with that woman, I wasn't particularly in the mood anymore myself. It sounds like she's really putting him through the wringer."

"What the heck were they fighting about?"

"I don't know. Something she was looking for at the apartment that she couldn't find? Something of hers she accused him of hiding someplace? I could hear him going through the closet, shoving things around and telling her over and over that he couldn't find it. I don't know what it was, but that's what happened."

"I'm sure whatever it is, it either doesn't exist or she has it."

"I know. I wanted to say that to him, too, but I didn't think he'd want to hear my opinion. I don't know her. And it would only sound like I was being nasty."

"At the end of the day, it's his situation, not yours."

"I know, but it affects me."

"Are you starting to …" She points to her chest, right over her heart.

I know better than to try to lie. "I would like to see if I can make things work with him. What's so bad about that?"

She rolls her eyes, very dramatic. "I won't bother giving you the whole song and dance about how you're supposed to be keeping it casual."

"Thank you very much."

"But you're supposed to be keeping it casual, you dork."

I lift my martini glass in salute. "You never let me down."

"I'm serious. You keep setting yourself up to be hurt."

"What was I supposed to do? I'm sorry, Hayley,

but I can't turn my emotions on and off like I'm a light switch. And I could understand if I'd flung myself at one of those guys on the dating site just because they happened to be a doctor and that happened to be who I was writing about right now. But I didn't. He found me, or I found him, and something happened. I can't explain what, but I know we both felt it, or he wouldn't have given me his number in the first place. I really like him. I'm not saying I'm falling in love or anything, but I really like him. For once, I would like for things to be simple. Is that too much to ask?"

She sighs, and now, she manages to look sympathetic. "Sweetie, I hate to tell you this, but there's no such thing as simple once you start getting a little older."

"I'm twenty-five, Hayley. The same as you."

"Yeah, and I already know of at least three girls we graduated with who are divorcing or already divorced."

"Seriously?"

"Seriously. Life moves fast. Plus, you're dating men older than we are. The older they get, the more history they're bound to have. Crazy exes. Children. Child support payments, weekend guests who smear peanut butter and jelly all over the place. Aging parents. Responsibilities."

It shouldn't come as a surprise that she makes a good point. She usually does.

"So, you're saying I should be the cool girl and

let this slide?" I ask, toying with my glass. Somehow, that doesn't feel quite right to me.

"What's so wrong with that?"

"I don't know." I shrug.

"You're pouting."

"Am not," I lie, pulling my bottom lip in where it belongs. "But I can't pretend it didn't bother me. He apologized a bunch of times, and I told him it was no big deal."

"He did apologize though," she points out, holding up a finger, which she then uses to signal a server.

The woman is magic, I swear. I could stand on a chair and wave my arms over my head until it looked like I was signaling planes to land, and I'd get nowhere. All she has to do is lift a finger.

"Yes, ladies?" He's cute and he gives Hayley that sort of special smile that I'm sure is supposed to be a signal. *Hey, baby, I'm off work in an hour. Meet me out back.*

He doesn't know Hayley. She is not the girl you meet out back.

"We'll need another round of drinks, an order of nachos, and four shrimp tacos." Once she's finished, she turns back to me, leaving him to do his job.

"You need to stop doing that," I warn as he walks away.

"Doing what?"

"Breaking hearts everywhere you go."

She scoffs, barely taking the time to shake her

head. "Anyway, all I'm saying is, if she's been away for a long time and there's still stuff between them that needs to be worked out, this sort of thing is to be expected."

My head hurts. I fold my arms on the table and rest it on top of them. "Why is everything so impossible?"

"Knock it off." She laughs. "It's not impossible. It's just life. Not everything is as perfect as it is in your books."

"But can't it be? Why can't it be?"

"Because what you write is fiction, my dear. Which is what separates it from reality. Reality stinks—which is why people flock to fiction, by the way. It's an escape. Really, you should be glad reality is such a kick in the nuts since that's why you have a career in the first place."

"Do you ever get tired of being right?" I groan.

"Nope. Being right is too much fun to get tired of. Now, sit up before I have no choice but to pour my water over you. Everything will be fine."

"Will it though?" I ask, lifting my head. Ordinarily, I wouldn't do what she ordered strictly on principle. Nobody tells me what to do.

But I know her. She's not above drowning me in the middle of a restaurant to prove a point.

"Sure, it will. This will blow over, and one day, you'll sit back and laugh over how dumb it was to ever let this Erin person get in your head."

"You should see her."

"No, thanks," she sighs, twirling her hair around one finger.

"She's beautiful. Like, almost as beautiful as you."

Hayley rolls her eyes.

"And brilliant. A surgeon. I don't know what kind exactly, but I know she was overseas on a research team for eight months. That's the sort of thing smart people do, right?"

"Smart people also write books that end up on the *New York Times* Best Sellers list," she reminds me. "Several times over, in case you forgot."

"She has a hold on him."

"She thinks he's a loser for changing his career path." My mouth falls open. "Well, she does!" she insists. "You already told me before that she dumped him because he'd changed things up, become less career-driven. That hasn't changed, so why would she?"

"It's obvious she wants him back."

"That's her problem."

"Oh, is it?" I ask as the server returns with our drinks. I make it a point to smile at him, which is a big change from the scowl I was just shooting at Hayley.

"Yes, it is," she hisses when we're alone again.

"When she's getting in the way of my good time, I have to say it's my problem too."

"It didn't have to be."

"You weren't there!" I practically shout.

A few people sitting at the bar turn to look at us.

Sorry, I mouth with a shrug.

"You could've expressed sympathy and laughed it off. I know; I know. It's easy for me to say. I wasn't there. Blah, blah, blah."

"Well, you weren't."

"Now, you know how to handle it should it ever happen again."

I snort. "It'd better not happen again."

"It'll probably happen again."

"I thought you were supposed to be making me feel better."

"Have you ever known me to shove smiley-faced platitudes down your throat for the sake of making you feel better?" she sighs.

"Good point."

And thankfully the nachos arrive when they do because I feel the sudden need to shove something into my mouth. Bonus: I can't blurt out anything idiotic when I'm busy crunching on tortilla chips and guacamole.

"Erin is the past. You are the future, if you choose to be. You're the girl he wants to spend time with now." She leans in, meeting my gaze while I shovel chips into my waiting mouth. "You're the girl he still wanted a hot make-out sesh with in your grandmother's pantry, even when he found out you weren't being honest with him."

I can't offer any stunning, cutting reply to that with a mouthful of food. There's nothing for me to do but mull it over while I chew. She's made a good point once again. He didn't have to be so accepting and willing to go along with things when he found out I might be writing about him. He had every right to tell me to stick it where the sun didn't shine.

But he didn't. And he wanted to see me again after that. Immediately after that in fact.

Maybe things aren't as bleak as I'm making them out to be. They rarely are. Whenever Hayley accuses me of being overdramatic, I fight like heck to convince her otherwise.

The truth? I know I can be. That's why I'm so good at writing romantic drama.

Or so I tell myself.

"So, you don't think I'm a step down from a hot, brilliant surgeon?" I ask, chewing my lip.

Hayley's eyes widen. "Jesus, is that what you think? Is that what has you worried?"

"Well … yeah. I thought that was pretty clear by the way I kept comparing myself to her."

"Oh, for heaven's sake." She puts her hands on the table, palms down, eyes burning holes in me. "Listen, because I'm not going to repeat myself. I don't care how hot she is. I don't care if she operates on brains or hearts or whatever it is. I don't care if she has a new procedure named after her. I don't care if she's a genius. She's not you."

"Like I'm so special?" I smirk.

She doesn't blink. "You are Kitty fucking Valentine. Yes, you're special. Now, eat the damn nachos and lighten up."

Who am I to argue when she makes such a strong point?

"I love you," I manage around a mouthful of refried beans and cheese.

She smiles. "I know. And you have cheese on your chin."

Chapter Seventeen

"WHEN'S THE LAST time you were out here?"

I have to think hard on that question as I climb out of Jake's very large, very shiny truck. It's refreshing—the fact that he doesn't drive some low-slung, sleek sports car.

Not that I have anything personal against sports cars or anything like that, but sometimes, a girl wants to stretch her legs a little. I'm not very tall, so for me to complain about legroom is saying something.

The sea breeze hits me right in the face, and instantly, all my worries drift away. There's nothing like a day at the beach to put life back into perspective.

"I wish I could remember," I admit, pulling a beach tote from the backseat. "It's been too long."

"It's the same for me," he admits. "I hope the boys can forgive me for not bringing them along, but I wanted to be able to focus on you today."

I know he's talking about the dogs, and it warms my heart to know he misses them and feels bad for leaving them at home.

"Next time," I suggest with a smile, which seems to perk him up.

The boardwalk is packed with people on a beautiful Sunday. No big surprise there, no more of a surprise than the sight of a rainbow of towels and umbrellas on the sand. It's not even officially summer yet, but the warm weather has everybody wishing it were.

Including me.

Cotton candy, French fries, pizza. So many intoxicating aromas hit me all at once, mixing with the salty sea breeze and the smell of sunscreen. There's nothing like the Jersey Shore. It's like a world of its own. Kids chase each other around, squealing and screaming. Teenagers try desperately to look cool as they wander from one store to another—they all sell the same T-shirts, so I don't get why there are so many versions of the same place. Older people walk slowly, strolling along and soaking it all in.

I identify most with them, I guess. It's enough to be out here, to be away from the computer for a little while.

"What do you think?" Jake asks as we step from the boardwalk to the warm sand. "Will this be enough to help clear your head?"

He suggested this excursion when I confessed to being stuck halfway through the book.

I have more than enough scenes plotted out in my head and on the page. It's just that I can't figure out how to get from one point to another. What do they say, these characters of mine? How do they feel? What are they trying to get through together? Sexy times are fine and wonderful, but there has to be a little more meat to make a compelling story.

"I hope so," I sigh with a weary smile.

"I don't know how you do it."

"What, write?" I ask while stumbling around behind him. I never did get the hang of walking gracefully through the sand, and it seems like I keep stepping on little bits of shells.

Jake, on the other hand, strolls along like he owns the entire stretch of beach. *What would it be like to have that sort of confiden*ce? And coordination, for that matter? "Yeah. It's a mystery to me."

"It's a mystery to me how you do what you do," I point out. "I mean, somebody comes into the ER, and you have to diagnose them. What do you do? Type their symptoms into a search bar and look at the results?"

"It's a little more than that." He laughs. I'm glad he didn't take it personally. "But I see what you mean."

"It takes all types of people to make the world. If we were all good at the same thing, life would be pretty boring, I guess."

He throws me a grin over his shoulder. "Have I ever told you how interesting you are?"

"Me?"

"Yeah, you." He comes to a stop. "This looks

like a good spot."

And it is—with enough space for us to stretch out, close enough to the water that we won't lose sight of our things if we go in.

I don't know if the people around us are going to be able to handle themselves once Jake takes off his shirt, however. Already, there are a handful of women—all ages, all sorts—eyeing us from their towels and chairs.

He's so completely unaffected by it. If there's anything I've learned from him, it's that devastatingly gorgeous people sometimes don't know how gorgeous they are. I've always figured in the back of my mind that they were aware and liked to pretend they weren't. Even Hayley, as long as I'm being honest. If I were as beautiful as she is, I'd never stop looking in a mirror, but she claims to have no idea why people look at her.

"You wanna go in?" he asks, nodding to the water.

The surf is fairly calm today, no dramatic crashing of waves. Instead of drawing people in though, there are only a smattering of swimmers out there.

"It might be a little too cold still." I grimace and then giggle. "I have my book. I'm good."

"Oh, come on." Darned if he doesn't pout for good measure. "Don't let me down. I was hoping I could get you out into the water."

"Why? Planning on drowning me?"

"No." He strips off his T-shirt, revealing the

body of a living, breathing god.

The sight of him slams into me like a speeding train, leaving me about as wrecked as I would be after getting hit for real. I can't even think for a second. My brain shuts down.

"N-no?" I whisper. The inside of my mouth is like sandpaper, which is funny since I could swear I'm salivating like one of Jake's dogs.

"No! Come on. Don't be a chicken." He wears a playful smirk as he turns away, trotting down to the water.

Now that his back is turned, the women around me can react openly to the sight of him. I'm pretty sure one of them faints, and another announces to her husband that she wants a divorce.

What am I supposed to do? Let him think I'm a chicken?

"Idiot, idiot, idiot," I mutter to myself as I take off my flowy cover-up to reveal a simple one-piece.

"Come on!" Jake calls out, already waist deep.

The instant the water hits my toes, I shriek and jump back. "It's freezing!" I scream.

"Not once you get used to it! Just jump in and let it hit you, and you'll get over it!" A wave hits him from behind, but he stands there like nothing happened. He's a brick wall, this guy.

Jump right in. Let it hit me. I'd say it was easy for him to say, but he's out there. He actually did it. And I wouldn't mind the excuse to get close to him with practically no clothes on.

Yes, Kitty. Do it for the muscles. You can grab his arms and shoulders and pretend you're doing it to keep from getting knocked over by the waves. Do it for the muscles.

The water hits me almost as hard as the sight of Jake without his shirt on. It's much less pleasurable than the sight of him, I can say that much.

Though the shock wears off pretty fast, and after that, the feeling of the water is exhilarating. Just as exhilarating as the feeling of Jake's arm as he grabs me by the waist and pulls me closer.

"See? Told you! I take an ice-cold shower every day, and I'm still alive."

"You plunge yourself into icy water every day?" I mean, adventure is one thing, but that seems to border on masochism.

"Yeah!" He dunks himself, leaning his head back so his hair slicks away from his face. When he straightens up, I could swear he's moving in slow motion. Or maybe that's a sign of my brain breaking down out of sheer overload. "It's like the first achievement of my day. Doing something I really, really don't wanna do. Living through it."

"Wait." I laugh, bobbing up and down in the salty water. "You don't want to do it, but you do?"

"It's a way of proving to myself that nothing's that bad. I can get through anything. Mind over matter, all that stuff."

He dunks himself again, and this time, he brings me with him. I pop out of the water, sputtering, which makes him laugh.

By the time we stumble out of the water, holding on to each other, my fingers and toes have pruned. But I wouldn't trade it for anything. When was the last time I played? When was the last time I dropped everything in favor of having fun?

I flop back onto the blanket with an ear-to-ear smile. "That was incredible."

He settles in next to me with a wry grin. "Hmm. You think that was incredible, you oughta see what I'm capable of."

Yes, I would like to see what he's capable of. I could've seen it before now, if it wasn't for a certain ex-girlfriend who couldn't leave well enough alone. The thought of her is like a cloud passing over the sun—it darkens my mood.

And he sees it right away. "I know I screwed up. I'm trying to make it up to you."

"I know." And I do. "So, what do you wanna do next? Do you like arcade games?"

"What do you think?" he asks, and that playful smile is back. "I think we should make it a competition. Whoever loses has to do something for the winner."

"Like what?" Something tells me I know what. He doesn't need to know I once spent an entire summer doing nothing but playing at the arcade or that my name was at the top of the leaderboard for Skee-Ball three weeks running.

"I'm sure we can come up with something," he

growls, and all of a sudden, I don't care about playing games.

We could find a nice, cozy truck, and he could bang my brains out inside. The fact that his truck is parked in the lot near the boardwalk just happens to fit my plan nicely.

Though public sex has never been on my list of to-dos, I'm sure Maggie would be delighted if she knew I was even considering this.

We pack things up and leave them in the truck, where Jake is enough of a gentleman to wait outside with his back turned while I change out of my suit and into a sundress. He does the same when I'm finished. Nobody wants to walk around in a damp bathing suit.

"We'll have to get a room next time," he announces on climbing out, combing his fingers through his hair. It's wild and wavy now that he's been in the ocean, a lion's mane I'd love to get tangled up in.

Next time. Yes, I can see there being a next time.

We're halfway down the boardwalk, strolling hand in hand and discussing pizza versus seafood when a scream cuts through the air.

I freeze, my hand tightening around Jake's. He's looking around, trying to figure out who's screaming. Before I know it, he drops my hand and takes off at full speed.

"Help me!" a woman screams while a teenage boy collapses on the boards.

There are a handful of concerned people crowding around now. Jake pushes his way through them while I bring up the rear.

"What happened?" he barks, kneeling by the boy.

"I think he's choking. I thought he was playing around," his mother wails, shaking the boy by the shoulders. "Wake up! Come on!"

"Let me," Jake insists, gently moving her out of the way.

The boy's skin is turning blue.

My heart's in my throat. *Is he dead?*

Jake pulls him up, sitting him upright, and then hauls him to his feet. "Come on. Cough it up," he mutters while linking his arms around the kid's waist and jamming his clenched fists against his midsection. Again. Again. "Come on, kid," Jake grunts.

Finally, the kid coughs, and roughly half a hot dog comes flying out onto the boards. His mom weeps, throwing her arms around both of them while the crowd cheers.

And I faint.

Chapter Eighteen

"KITTY. KITTY? WAKE up."

But I don't want to. It's so nice and cool and quiet with my eyes closed.

"Kitty. Wake up."

Somebody's smacking my cheeks.

"Hey," I whisper, turning my head from one side to the other. "Knock that off."

"There she is." Somebody kisses my forehead and laughs. "Open your eyes before I throw you back in the ocean."

That gets through to me, and my eyes fly open. I hear people laughing softly around me and wonder who the heck they are and why they're here.

Wait. Where is here?

Right. It takes a second for me to get my bearings, but once I do, it all becomes clear. I'm in Jake's arms, under a covered shelter on the boardwalk. The people who laughed are nosy spectators who had watched me faint after watching Jake save that kid's life.

"How is he?" I ask, pushing hair away from my face. My knees hurt; it takes a quick glance at them to show me why. I skinned them a little when I went down.

"He?" Jake asks with a frown, and then the confusion clears. "Oh, he's fine. A little shaken up, I guess, but his mom took him away someplace. Maybe back to their motel if they're staying here. I don't know. I was a little more concerned about you."

He hands me a bottle of water. "Here. Somebody gave me this when you were out." He uncaps it and then practically lifts it to my mouth, though I'm already holding it.

"I think I can manage," I whisper with a faint smile. "But thank you."

"Sorry. It's a habit. Taking care of people I care about and all that."

I can't shake the memory of that boy. "You saved his life. He was blue, but you saved him."

"He was choking. It's a pretty common thing."

"Yeah, but nobody else thought to do it. Not even his mother."

"You'd be surprised how rare it is for an immediate family member to get it together in enough time to jump in and help," he explains. His arm is around my shoulders, which is nice. His touch comforts me. "It's usually a bystander. We don't have any skin in the game."

"There weren't any bystanders helping either," I point out.

They just stood there, staring, not helping at all.

The way I did.

All this gets me is a shrug of his shoulders. "I don't know what to say. I knew what to do, and I did it. I didn't think. I acted."

"That's really special."

He shakes his head. "Not really."

"Yes, really! If we found that kid's mom right now, I bet she'd tell you exactly how special it was. You saved her son's life when nobody else did anything. She has him now because of you." My hand finds his and holds on tight. "I think that's what made me faint. I was overwhelmed for everybody."

"How are you feeling now?"

I get the sense that he doesn't want to keep talking about it. Like it embarrasses him. He doesn't want me to think of him as a hero. Which is why I let up on the subject.

"Better. I'm still hungry."

His relief is obvious when he smiles. "Yeah, me too."

Though before we sit down to eat, he makes it a point to stop at a little store selling various first aid products and picks up antibiotic ointment and bandages for my knees.

Not my most attractive look. Not by a long shot. But how am I supposed to resist when he's so determined to take care of me?

It's sort of a challenge for the rest of the day, not staring up at him in awe.

He saved a kid's life.

He literally saved a kid's life.

The kid could've died right there.

Jake saved him.

I mean, I usually have to stop myself from gaping at him in complete wonder as it is, and that was before he saved somebody's life in front of me. Only knowing how much he'd hate it stops me.

We spend the rest of the day eating pizza slices as big as our heads, playing Skee-Ball—I beat him handily in eight out of ten rounds; it's not even close—and walking up and down the boardwalk. There are all sorts of silly things to do, like dressing up in old-timey clothes and having pictures taken or going on crazy, extreme rides that turn my stomach from just watching other people on them.

"Come on," he begs, pointing to one of those slingshots that flings people way high up into the air.

"I don't think so." I laugh, shaking my head.

"You only live once!"

"I just ate my weight in pizza. Do you really want to be sitting next to me when that thing shoots us into the air, and I hurl up the contents of my stomach?"

"Hmm. Good point."

"Next time," I promise, sliding my arm around his as we continue walking.

Yes, I can definitely see there being a next time. I can almost imagine us bringing our kids down during the summer, staying at some kitschy motel—or better yet, a condo—the little ones taking turns riding on Jake's shoulders as we—

Hold it, Valentine. I can practically hear Hayley's voice in my head, and somehow, the brilliant late afternoon sunshine dims a little. *What are you thinking? You'd better pump the brakes—fast.*

I know she—or rather, my subconscious—is right. I know I have to play it smart. We haven't even slept together or made this thing of ours official, and I'm letting one little lifesaving maneuver seal the deal. I can't let myself fall in love.

"I have to ask you something." He stops, bringing me to a halt with him. The fact that he looks serious doesn't exactly make me feel smiley and confident.

"What is it?" *Please, don't spoil our perfect day.* I mean, I fainted and skinned my knees, but it was perfect otherwise.

"Is that whole Heimlich thing going to be in your book?"

I have to laugh until I realize he's serious. "I haven't thought about it yet. What, do you think I'm always taking notes for my current project?"

"Aren't you? I'm not trying to be a jerk. I'm curious. I don't know how it works."

"If I went around, taking notes all the time, I could never live in the moment." I shrug. "That's as much as I can say. I haven't thought about my book all day, which I guess is a good thing. Wasn't I supposed to get my head out of my work and enjoy myself?"

"That was the general point." He tucks a strand of hair behind my ear, letting his fingertips linger on my cheek before bending down for a kiss that pretty much melts me.

"Careful," I whisper once he lets me come up for air. "I'll end up fainting again."

"I'll catch you this time," he promises with a smile before leaning down for another kiss.

THERE'S ONLY ONE thing that could ruin the mood as we reach Manhattan, parking in a lot not far from my building and walking up to my floor. Only one thing could take what's been a virtually perfect day, which is clearly leading into a perfect night, and turn it on its head.

"Oh, hi." Matt's just coming out with Phoebe as I approach my door with Jake's hand in mine.

Don't you dare. Don't you stinking dare. I will straight-up kill you if you ruin this.

Can he hear my thoughts? Of course he can't, but that doesn't mean he can't smirk like he knows exactly where the night's about to go.

I would really like to know what gives him the right. I truly would. *Do I ever smirk at the skanks he parades in and out? No.* Okay, sure, I played marching band music that one time when he was in the middle of sex, but at least he took the hint—or seemed to. There hasn't been nearly as much moaning and screaming coming from his apartment since then.

Jake, ever the good guy, immediately crouches to greet Phoebe. "What a beauty." He smiles as he scratches her behind the ears.

"Thank you." *Why is it that pet owners take compliments like that personally? He didn't give birth to the dog.* "You a dog owner?"

"I have a pair of huskies who'd love to make her acquaintance." Jake leans in like he's telling Phoebe a secret. "They're fixed, so you wouldn't have to worry about it."

"So is she." Matt laughs.

So, he can put the nice guy act on for a stranger. How great for him.

He looks us both over. "You've been at the beach today, huh?"

Wow. What a genius. I'm carrying a tote bag with sand stuck to it.

"Yeah, it was beautiful out there." Jake beams. "Just perfect. You get out to the beach much?"

Why are we standing here, talking to Matt? Why, when there are other things we could—and most certainly should—be doing? If only Jake knew what a dick Matt's been lately—and how he assumed Jake only went to Grandmother's party so he could get in my pants.

I didn't tell him about that—of course because I am a mature, rational person and not a tattletale. Yes, I know how stupid that sounds.

It's just that I've never been a fan of two-faced people, and that's how Matt strikes me right now. He's all smiles and laughs to Jake's face, but I know what he's said behind Jake's back. *How can he even look at me right now, knowing that I know?*

"You okay?" Jake asks.

Terrific. Put the spotlight on me. I've never been good at hiding my feelings behind a happy face.

He turns to Matt. "She went out on me for a few minutes today. Too much sun maybe."

"You fainted?" Matt asks with a frown.

"I'm okay, really. I think I was overwhelmed." I nudge Jake with my elbow. "I had never watched somebody being brought back from the brink of death before."

"What?" Now, Matt's truly lost.

"A kid was choking, and I helped him. No big deal," Jake insists. Maybe it's the amount of sun he got today, but he looks a little red-faced.

"I see," Matt muses with his eyes on me. "I guess watching somebody being so heroic would make a girl swoon."

"We've gotta go, and I'm sure Phoebe does too." I have the door open and the two of us inside the apartment before I even finish speaking, calling out, "Have a good night!" as I close and lock the door between us.

"What was that about?" Jake whispers, snickering. "I remember the two of you bickering when I first saw you in the ER."

"Yeah, he's a pest," I sigh.

And I sincerely hope Jake can forget about him.

Only he can't, not right away. "He strikes me as being protective of you. Like a brother."

"You think so?" I truly wish we could stop talking about him.

Was this how Jake felt when I wanted to talk about his Glamazon of an ex-girlfriend? Now, I feel bad for not letting the subject drop when he asked me to.

Though Matt's not an ex. He's hardly even a friend. Friends aren't mean the way he is or so critical. It's one thing for Hayley to be that way. We've been friends for years, like sisters.

"Yeah. You didn't sense him sizing me up?" Jake chuckles, good-natured. "I guess that's nice. You live across the hall from somebody who cares whether you're happy."

"I don't know if I'd go that far. But as neighbors go, I could do worse."

It occurs to me that I have no idea what to do next. We're here, in my apartment which I cleaned from top to bottom in preparation, hoping this moment would come soon.

Only now that the moment is here, I don't know how to move things along. It was one thing to jump him on his sofa, but starting from square one after Matt put a damper on my spirits is proving to be a challenge.

In short, I don't feel sexy. At all.

Does he sense it? Does he feel it when he comes to

me, looping his arms around my waist?

"We had a long day," he murmurs. "It's only seven o'clock, and I'm wrung out."

"I think I am too," I admit. Sure, let him think it's only fatigue and too much sun and not my sudden loss of confidence.

"Maybe we should rest for a while," he suggests. "If that's not too forward of me."

"Not at all."

No, it's perfect. Absolutely perfect. Once again, he saves the day.

And when we wake up—preferably in my bed, preferably all wrapped up in each other—it's on. It's so on.

I am going to rock his world.

Chapter Nineteen

MY TONGUE'S STUCK to the roof of my mouth, and I'm pretty sure I drooled all over Jake's chest.

Not the best start.

"Oh jeez," I groan, pulling myself up and away from him. "What hit me? What time is it?"

There's a little bit of gray light coming in through the window, but that's as much as I know.

Jake stirs, reaching blindly for the phone he left on my nightstand before we both passed out. A day in the ocean is like a sleeping pill for me—for both of us, it seems.

"Oh shit!" He jumps up before I'm even fully out of his way. "It's five thirty!"

"In the morning?" I ask, horrified.

I don't think either of us moved the entire time we were asleep. I drifted off with my head against his chest, and that's how I was when I woke up.

"Yes! I have to be at the hospital in an hour, and I never got home to take care of the dogs. Damn it." He thrusts his feet into his shoes while pulling a shirt over his head. "They probably pissed all over the apartment and tore the couch to shreds."

I can't help but wonder if he blames me for this. "I'm sorry," I murmur, sitting in a nest of blankets on the bed. "I should've set an alarm."

"No, no," he grumbles. "It's my fault. I didn't expect to sleep for, what, ten hours? Is there some sort of gas leak in this apartment? Or did you drug me or something?"

I'm maybe seventy percent sure he's only kidding as I scramble to follow him out of the room. "I'm really sorry. I was hoping—it doesn't matter." Now's not the time to babble about the sex I was hoping we'd have.

"Yeah. Me too." He kisses my forehead while unlocking the door. "I'll call you when I can, as soon as I can. I'm sorry to run like this."

He's already down the hall by the time I say good-bye. I doubt he heard me.

But somebody else did. Matt opens his door—because of course he does—and takes in the sight of me in my oversize T-shirt with a smirk. He's seen me in less—not that I'm proud of that or anything—so I don't bother putting on a modest act even though he is well-groomed and has actual clothes on.

"Yes?" I ask with a smile.

"I heard the commotion out here and thought I'd check and make sure everything's okay." Yes, because he's just sitting down to get his workday started, the busy little bee who lives across the hall.

"Everything's fine. He overslept, is all."

I can't help myself. *Should I do this? I'm doing this.*

Stretching, I grin. "Guess I tired him out."

He takes one look at me and lowers his brow. "Liar."

"I'm not lying."

"You didn't do anything."

"Who says?"

"Me and the wall between our apartments."

If only I had something near my hand that I could throw in his general direction. "Oh? What, were you waiting all night, listening? Like a pervert?"

"No, but considering that there are times when I can actually hear you typing, I'd at least expect to hear bedsprings creaking. Something."

"Maybe we did it on the floor."

"Maybe he's not as much of a superman as he looks," he counters. "Because floor, bed, or otherwise, neither of you made a sound."

"We're discreet."

"You're lying." He laughs. "So what? Why pretend? You didn't fuck."

"You're disgusting."

"Oh, I forgot who I was talking to." He gasps, hands folded over his chest. "You didn't make sweet, passionate love that, like, united your souls in an eternal bond."

He's still laughing as I close the door.

Jerk.

Now, I'm wide-awake after, frankly, sleeping like a log. I feel alert and ready to go now that my heart rate has already skyrocketed, thanks to Jake freaking out and running around like the place was on fire.

After yoga and a shower, I sit down with a smoothie and decide to get to work. I might as well, right? At this rate, I could hit my word count for the day before noon and spend the rest of the day not feeling guilty.

I have to write a scene where they're at the beach. I just have to. What happened yesterday is too perfect to be left unexplored. Sure, some of the details need changing, but the general hero thing needs to be part of this book. It just does.

Maybe somebody almost drowns? Sure, and their family member or friend drags them out of the water, but they're unresponsive. And my doctor hero, Jeff, has to perform CPR to save them.

Ooh, that sounds good. I can hardly keep myself from pounding away on the keys, building the scene.

A beach. A beautiful day. My heroine is too busy admiring her hero's incredible, tanned body to notice somebody is flailing around in the water.

"What's that?" Jeff stood, sunscreen forgotten.

Nikki jumped up behind him, still rubbing lotion into his skin.

"What's what?" she asked, distracted.

Who wouldn't be distracted with all this ... Jeff in

front of them? He was in a class of his own, a walking, talking fantasy. There could be a shark out in the water, and she wouldn't notice.

He took a few steps toward the water's edge, leaving her standing on her own. Now, she could see what he was talking about—and it was enough to nearly stop her heart.

Somebody was in trouble.

Jeff took off without a second thought, feet pounding the sand, running for the surf, and diving in. The drowning man wasn't alone out there. Somebody was already pulling him in, waving an arm over their head to signal for help between strokes through the water.

Once Jeff reached them, the process went a lot faster. Nikki watched, frozen in shock as Jeff dragged the man onto the sand. He was unconscious, eyes closed, body limp. People came from all directions, crying out in surprise, hands over their mouths. A few of them turned their kids away, like they didn't want them to see what might happen.

Jeff paid no attention. He tilted the man's head back, pinched off his nose, and blew into his mouth before performing chest compressions. Again. Again. He worked without looking around, without asking questions. A man with a mission. Determined, just like she knew he could be once he set his mind on something.

Only this time, it didn't seem like determination would be enough. Nikki wiped a tear from her eye with a hand that still smelled like sunscreen. What would it do to Jeff if this man didn't—

Suddenly, the man coughed, water shooting up out of

his mouth. Jeff rolled him onto his side, letting him cough it out while the crowd around him cheered.

Nikki didn't cheer. All she could do was stand there, feet stuck in the sand, watching as the man she now knew she loved refused to accept thanks for saving a stranger's life.

Okay, so I changed things up quite a bit. But that's how it has to be. I can't let the scenario reflect real life too closely. Jake inspired me, and that's enough.

Another thing that will change: Nikki won't faint like I did.

Instead, she'll take Jeff back to the room they rented for the weekend and screw his brains out, the way I wanted to do with Jake.

The way I could've done if I hadn't fallen dead asleep. Then again, so did he. I guess I have that effect on men.

How'd it go last night? Hayley's text waits for me once I pull myself away from the scene to fill my water bottle. There are plenty of winky emojis, followed by a few eggplants and peaches.

Are you asking whether he put it in my butt? I text back.

Hey, it's possible. Not probable, but possible.

I have to laugh. Not probable at all. There are certain things I'd need a lot of time and preparation for, and I still doubt I'd ever go through with it. But that's what boundaries are for.

Try not to be too disappointed. We fell asleep and didn't wake up until he had to leave for work.

She's typing an instant later, the three dots blinking on her side of the screen. *Oh boy, I'm in for it.* It's taking her much too long to come up with something.

Boo! What's his problem? He can't stay awake long enough to bone you? How old is he? Does he have grandkids?

You've seen his picture, I remind her, referring to a shot I snapped and shared with her when we were out with the dogs. You know that's not a problem. *We were gonna take a nap and do it after, but …*

She sends me a cringing emoji. *Big mistake. Never take the sex nap.*

Well, I know that now.

I wish there'd been a reason for her to tell me before. Some things you can't know until you're in that situation. I know I'd never think to warn somebody against taking a pre-sex nap.

When the phone goes off again, I'm ready to tell Hayley to leave her opinions to herself, that I have the whole sex thing well in hand. I don't have it well in hand, but I will. Soon. Just as soon as the stars align and nobody falls asleep and nobody calls at the wrong moment.

No biggie.

Only it's not Hayley. It's Jake. Good thing I'm not superstitious, or I'd think he knew we were talking about him. Just how he'd know that, I haven't the first clue. But the coincidence is uncanny.

Sorry about this morning. Can I come by later today? Around six maybe?

Can he?

You'd better, I reply before doing a little happy dance. *Yes. This is good. This is gonna happen. I'm gonna rock his world, just like I've imagined doing way too many times.*

The promise of what's coming later makes writing my next scene easier. The motel room sexathon, where Nikki throws her inhibitions to the wind. It's easy to get super dirty in a place that's not home. And this time, there's no threat of patients or coworkers coming in to interrupt them.

I'm so into it that I hardly notice the way time flies by. When the doorbell rings, I'm stunned to find that it's almost six o'clock.

Wow. If the thought of Jake coming over wasn't enough to get me excited, imagining the two of us in a motel room where we broke the bed certainly did it. My engine is all kinds of revved up as I hurry to the door.

"Hi—" It's all I manage to get out of my mouth before Jake's all over me, closing the door with his foot while picking me up off the floor in those strong, firm arms of his.

"Now," he growls between kisses, "let's not make the mistake of falling asleep this time."

Chapter Twenty

"WAIT, WAIT!" I'M laughing as he carries me to the bedroom with his arms around my waist, kissing my chin and mouth and neck and throat. "Wait a second!"

"I can't wait. I've been dying all day, thinking about you and what I missed out on." He pushes me back onto the bed, making me squeal before pulling his shirt over his head and dropping it on the floor.

"I've been thinking about you too," I whisper as he crawls on top of me, taking his time, eyes locked with mine. "All day."

"Oh?" He finds the pulse in my throat and flicks his tongue over it. My head falls back. "What were you thinking?" he whispers before taking another lick of my sensitive skin.

"All kinds of things," I confess as his hands work their way under my shirt.

I sit up, arms over my head so he can pull it off and toss it aside. He cups my breasts, tasting them, while I run my fingers through his hair and hold his head close. So close.

"Dirty things?" he asks, now working on my jeans.

I wiggle my hips, and he slides them down before devouring my legs, running his hands over them while kissing his way from ankle to knee—before moving further north.

I lie back on the bed, eyes closing, as his tongue works all sorts of magic along my inner thighs. "Dirty things," I whisper, lifting my hips again so he can discard my panties.

My God, this is happening. This is finally happening. This sex god is in my room, in my bed, about to worship me. *I am glorious. I am a goddess.* He's been thinking about me all day, and he can't wait to finish what we keep trying to start.

"Beautiful," he whispers, his breath hot against my most private parts.

Before I know it, my thighs are gripping his head, and I'm riding out an exquisite orgasm while his skillful tongue takes me over the edge.

I'm still coming down from it, gasping for air and moaning his name as he opens a foil packet and gets himself ready. He's hard, so hard, so ready for me. *For me! He wants me!* Even with my head in a fog of pleasure, I can't help but want to pinch myself. This has to be a dream.

I don't want it to end.

I work my way back on the bed to give him room, my head on the pillows, and I take him in my arms when he lowers himself over me. There's heat here, yes, the sort of heat that threatens to burn me up.

But there's something else. Something sweeter, more tender, something deeper than that. This is Jake. Jake is just about everything I could ask for and more.

"I don't think I can wait much longer," he admits before kissing me deeply.

I tangle my fingers in his hair, opening my legs wider to take him in. There's so much of him.

He breaks the kiss, his mouth close to my ear, and he reaches down to guide himself into me. I close my eyes, holding on tight, ready to take him in.

He groans just a split second before pushing forward. "Erin …" he breathes.

Whoa.

Wait.

My eyes fly open when I realize what he just said. There's no way I imagined that, no matter how much I want to believe I did.

"What?" I whisper in his ear. My fingers press into his shoulders. "What did you say?"

He knows he said it too. I can tell. His body has gone stiff on top of mine, like if he doesn't move, I'll forget he's there. But let's face it; there's way too much of him for me to forget his presence.

Especially now that I can't breathe with his weight on top of me, unmoving. I try to push him, palms against his chest, but I might as well be trying to lift an elephant.

Finally, I have to gasp, "Get off!"

And he does, and I slide away, so I can get air into my lungs.

It's more than that. Much more. I need to put at least a few inches between us while I figure out what the heck just happened. I pull the sheets over me while I'm at it since I've never felt so exposed in all my life.

Jake, meanwhile, is facedown on the bed, his head buried in the pillow to my right. His fists are clenched on either side.

I don't know what to do. *Should I say something? Tell him it's okay? That it happens?*

This has never happened to me before.

Heck, it might've been easier to deal with if he'd lost his erection or something. Sure, his ego would sting, but we wouldn't both be left with the knowledge that he was thinking about somebody else while he was moments away from being inside me.

I could hear a pin drop; it's so silent. I'm almost afraid to breathe.

Until a shriek cuts through the air, so sudden and unexpected that it makes me jump. And another shriek. More and more, overlapping each other, screaming women and the sound of harsh, screeching violins.

"What the hell?" Jake shouts as the noise gets louder and louder, filling the room.

Screaming and screeching and shrieking like …

A horror movie.

Oh, he didn't. I mean, he clearly did, the louse. I should've been waiting for him to retaliate.

And oh, his timing is impeccable.

I stomp over to the wall between my apartment and Matt's and pound my fist against it. "Enough!" I shout with my mouth near the wall. "You've made your point!"

The apartment goes silent again.

"What was that about?" Jake asks.

I'm still facing the wall. "Long story. Sort of a silent war."

"Not so silent."

"True."

We stay like that for a while until I remember I'm stark naked. If the man in my bed hadn't just whispered the name of his ex-girlfriend, it wouldn't be a big deal. I mean, he was all over me a few minutes ago.

Now? I'm exposed and uncomfortable. Incredible how a single four-letter word can turn everything upside down.

"What am I supposed to do?" I have to whisper after an eternity of this, neither of us moving or speaking. "Tell me what to do here. I'm completely lost."

He doesn't say anything. Here I am, with a man who seems to always have something to say, some bit of positive advice or a lighthearted quip. Some piece of wisdom. And he's just as lost as I am.

"I guess …" he whispers, barely lifting his face from the pillow, his voice muffled as a result. "I guess it would be too much to ask for you to forget that just happened."

"Yeah, I don't think I can do that," I admit. "I wish I could. I do."

"I know. Me too." He finally rolls onto his side, facing me. "I'm mortified. I can't believe that happened. I am so, so sorry."

"I know." It's amazing—the fact that I'm able to speak when there's so much pressure building in my chest. This time, it has nothing to do with his weight on top of me.

"I swear, I didn't mean for it to happen."

"I get it," I whisper with my head bobbing up and down. I can't look at him. I'll die if I look at him. It's easier to stare at the wall.

"She's not even part of my life anymore."

See, there are certain things even I can't excuse. Evidently, this is one of them.

My T-shirt is on the floor not far from my feet, so I reach down and pull that over my head if only to regain a little dignity. "That's obviously untrue or else you wouldn't have groaned her name while the two of us were about to have sex. She's on your mind. She's part of your mind still."

My legs are shaking, but I stand my ground anyway. Whatever it takes so long as I don't have to remain in bed with him.

Could I handle this better? I wish that question wouldn't come up as I put on my panties, which he flung across the room. *Should I be the cool girl? Should I laugh it off?*

No. I can't believe that's the right answer, and I'd have an entire earful to give to the person who tried to convince me otherwise. Being the cool girl and laughing this off and acting like it doesn't mean anything would be the same as sweeping a problem under the rug and pretending it doesn't exist.

This is a problem. A very big problem, far too large to fit under a rug. A problem named Erin.

When am I going to start listening to my instincts rather than brushing them aside?

"Can we talk about it?" he asks from the bed.

The rustling of the sheets and creaking of the springs tell me he's sitting up. I can only rely on my ears since turning his way would mean showing him the tears in my eyes. I would rather not do that.

"What is there to say?"

Where are my jeans? I have to find my jeans. I have to keep moving because if I stop, I might fall apart.

I don't love him. I'm not in love with him.

But darn it, I could've been. This could've been something special. Or so I told myself.

"That it didn't mean anything?"

That shouldn't strike me as funny, but I laugh anyway. "Come on. That's the oldest line in the book."

The jeans are poking out from under the bed. One of us must've kicked them aside. I reach for them.

"It's the truth."

"Stop lying to yourself. Just stop in general." Now, I have to look at him because he's starting to frustrate me worse than he already has.

He's devastated. I can read it in every line of his face, like the ones between his eyebrows and at the corners of his eyes. He looks like a man in pain.

"I didn't want this to happen," he whispers.

"I know you didn't. Neither did I." I have to sit. My knees are watery. There's a little chair not far from the bed, near the window, and I plop into it with my hands pressed together between my knees.

"It really is over between us," he offers. "I want you to know that."

"You don't have to—"

"I mean it," he insists. "It's way over. It has been—"

"For months. Over a year even," I finish for him. "I know that. But there's over, and there's over. You might not be dating her, but she's on your mind." I can't say more than that because that would mean admitting the very real possibility that Dr. Erin is still part of his heart too.

He runs both hands through his hair before holding his head between them. "I told myself she was gone. I want her to be gone."

"Listen, it happens." *Am I honestly comforting him*

right now? Am I trying to make him feel better? "She went away. You didn't get the opportunity to close things off. Sometimes, distance helps things, but then she came back. And now, all those months might as well have never happened."

He heaves a sigh, his back expanding and contracting in time. "How are you so smart about this? You're not even a part of it, but you see it so much clearer than I do."

Not a part of it? I'd say the fact that the memory of his ex-girlfriend kept me from getting laid and pretty much ruined whatever we had been building together most definitely puts me smack dab in the middle.

But that's neither here nor there. I get his point anyway.

"It's always easier to see things when you're standing outside," I offer in a soft voice. "Besides, this is the sort of stuff I deal with for a living. You can jump in and perform the Heimlich maneuver on a kid whose mother panicked and forgot what to do. I can see your problems clearly because I'm not the one involved, and it's my job to understand why people feel the way they do."

"I guess you're right." He drops his hands and looks at me. "What now?"

Is he trying to kill me?

"Now? I think you should get your clothes on and go home—or wherever you need to go. But home might be best. Do some thinking, play with the dogs. But you need to figure this out."

"I don't want to say good-bye to you," he whispers. "Not now. Not for good either."

"Who says it has to be for good?" I ask with a shaky chuckle. This is killing me. I can't take it, but I don't have a choice. "I only suggested you think things through. You need to work it out for yourself. I can't do it for you. Neither can Erin." Her name makes my mouth feel sour, like I just tasted fresh lemon juice. Or bile.

"You're right. I have to think this through. I never imagined …"

"I get it." And I do. I don't have to like it though. "Get dressed. I'll wait out in the living room." Or in the kitchen, where there happens to be a collection of liquor bottles, most of them unopened.

Something tells me that's going to change tonight.

So stupid. So, so stupid. I knew he was still stuck on her. Why else would he have answered the phone when she called, even when we were on the verge of taking our clothes off and getting freaky? Why would he have spent so much time fighting on the phone with her when he knew I was waiting in the other room?

Because he's still in love with her—or at least because there's too much unfinished business between them. She dumped him and left the country. He didn't exactly have the chance to get right with things.

His footsteps shuffle out behind me after just a few minutes. "I, uh, guess I'd better go."

"Okay." I'm standing by the window, arms wrapped around myself, staring out at the street below. Nobody down there knows what it means to be me right now, disappointed and sad and embarrassed over something I didn't even do.

"Can I …" He takes a few steps closer. "Can I call you?"

"Sure." I shrug, trying to sound upbeat and failing miserably. "Give me a little time though. Okay?"

"Yeah. I'm sorry."

"I know." I can't give him more than that.

I've already given him more than a lot of women would in my position. Some girls would've thrown him out and tossed his clothes behind him, not even giving him the time to get dressed. Some would've shouted at him, called him every name in the book for even daring to think of another woman while in bed with them.

Not that I don't want to. Not that I don't want to make him feel as small as he unwittingly made me feel. But I'm not that person. I can't do that to him. I still like him so darn much.

That might be the worst part of all.

At least I manage to wait to cry until the door closes with a soft click.

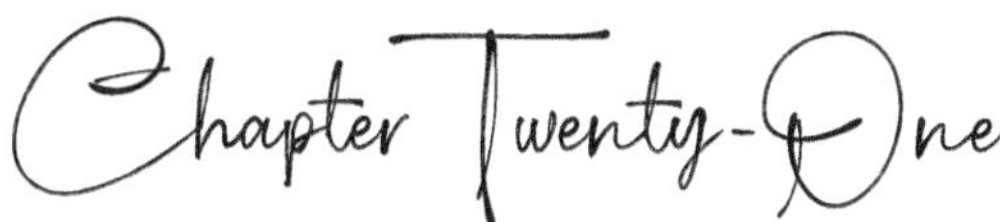

Chapter Twenty-One

"HELLO, MR. PATRÓN. We meet again."

I pour myself a shot in spite of my pledge to never, ever drink tequila again after the total mess I made of myself last time. When I got blackout drunk while trying to muster up the courage to write a measly sex scene.

To think, that used to be a problem. Now, I have my characters tying each other to the bedposts with sheets, for heaven's sake. Amazing what I can come up with, given the right inspiration.

Jake was my inspiration.

I down the shot in one quick swallow and welcome the warm sensation it sends through me, down my throat, through my chest. The chest Jake was only just kissing, touching …

"Stop it," I warn myself as I pour another shot.

Is there enough liquor in the world to get him out of my mind?

No. Not him. Only the memory of what just happened. Yes, I could stand to forget that. Permanently.

I almost want to text Hayley and tell her I was

right. He was stuck on Erin all along. I wasn't enough to get her out of his head or his heart. Because I'm not enough, period.

I should know that by now.

The third shot's a little saltier, thanks to the tears rolling down my cheeks and soaking my face in general.

Stupid men. Stupid ex-girlfriends.

Stupid me.

I care too much. I want him too much. I want us desperately, but that's not going to happen. Not now. Probably not ever. I mean, how would I ever feel comfortable with him again? How could I ever stop asking myself if he's thinking about me or about the brilliant, driven surgeon who broke his freaking heart?

My hand strays toward the bottle again, but I stop myself this time. I'm still capable of restraint. The alcohol hasn't worked its full magic yet, so my good sense hasn't been completely overshadowed.

Besides, I'm angry now. Angry with Jake and with myself and with the entire freaking world because if this is what it takes to be a successful author in today's market, I don't want any part of it. I'm not cut out for this.

I can't call Maggie and chew her out over it.

I can't do that to Hayley either.

There's only one more option.

Moments later, I'm pounding the side of my fist against Matt's front door. "I know you're home, so don't bother trying to pretend you're not!" I call out before banging again.

"Easy, easy!" He flings the door open, scowling. "I had to crate Phoebe since I figured you'd be pissed."

"I am pissed," I hiss. "I'm pissed at you."

"I wouldn't expect anything less."

"This is all your fault. You and men like you." I jab a finger against his chest. "You're the kind of guy who does this sort of thing, aren't you? Telling a girl one thing when you're thinking something else. How do you sleep at night?"

"Hang on." He takes my wrist in his hand to keep me from poking a hole in his chest. "This isn't about the sound effects I played?"

"No," I scoff, waving my free hand. *Oh boy.* The hallway's starting to tip on its side. Not a good sign. I have to steady myself, or he's never going to take me seriously.

"What's wrong then? Why are you assaulting me? Where's Dr. Muscles?"

"He's gone, okay? He's gone and he's never coming back and I hope you're happy." A tear threatens to fall, but I blink it back.

I want to scream. I want to punch a hole in the wall. I can feel it building inside me. Fury. Rage. I could tear down this whole building because, darn it, life isn't fair.

Instead of screaming, all I can do is whisper, "Why am I never enough?"

He blinks hard and then shakes his head a little like he's shaking the cobwebs loose. "Why … what?"

"Me." I jab a finger into my chest this time. "Why am I never enough?"

"Enough for what?"

"Enough for a man to want me. Just me. Not his job, not his ex-girlfriend. Me."

"Ah, Christ." He shakes his head with a sigh. "Come in. Pet a dog. You'll feel better."

"It's not something Phoebe can help," I whisper, though I walk into his apartment anyway.

Why not? It's not a good thing to drink alone. I've heard that one too many times. There has to be some truth to it.

Though doesn't that mean the other person's supposed to be drinking too? Hmm. I'll have to look that up later.

"Sit." He points me to the couch.

"Where are you going?" I ask as I cross the room. How come it's so big? *My apartment doesn't feel this big. I'm dizzy.*

I drank more than I should have. Again.

Pull it together, girl. I sit up a little straighter and smooth my shirt and hair down.

He'll never let me live it down if I make a mess like I did before.

"I'm getting water and ibuprofen for you," he calls out from the kitchen.

"I'll be okay."

"With the water and ibuprofen," Matt insists.

"Bossy."

"Yeah, well, take it from somebody who's battled through many a hangover." He comes back with two bottles—water and pills—and puts them in my hands.

"Thanks," I mumble. "I can't open the pills right now though."

"Too drunk?"

"No." I hold up the water bottle. "This is in my other hand."

"Oh, man. You're blitzed." He does it for me and then opens the water. "Here."

Then, he lets Phoebe out of her crate before sitting down with me, pulling a box of tissues onto the couch with us. "So … is that what happened with the doctor? He's still in love with his ex?"

"I think so. I had a feeling he was, but I told myself to ignore it. Hayley told me to ignore it too. She told me I was better than that girl. I knew she was wrong."

"Don't be so hard on yourself."

"It's obviously true, Matt. I'm not good enough. Once again," I sigh before a tear falls. "Crap. Now, I'm crying."

"Which is why I brought the tissues out." He nudges the box in my direction.

"I don't want to cry."

"Sometimes, it doesn't matter whether you wanna cry or not. You just do. I won't tell anybody."

"Fine. I might cry. It's gonna get ugly."

"You've thrown up on me. I can handle tears."

"He said her name, you know," I whisper as another tear falls and then another one. "When we were, like, in the middle of sliding into home base." I'm dying. Only tequila would get me to admit something so humiliating.

His jaw drops. "He didn't."

"He did."

"Oh my God. What a dumb thing to do. That's, like, basic stuff. You don't say the name of the ex. Ever, if possible."

"Welp, he did." I blow my nose, probably too loudly. "And that was sorta the end of that."

"No kidding." He snorts.

I glance at him from the corner of my eye. "You don't think I was wrong?"

"Wrong? For what?"

"For telling him he should go home and think things over?"

"Hell no!" He even laughs. "Uh, if you didn't tell him to leave, I would have to wonder if you were half as smart as I thought you were."

"You think I'm smart?"

"Of course that's what you would latch on to." He snickers. "Yeah. You have your moments. It was right to have him leave. It's not like you two were a serious couple and this was something to, like, go to therapy over. Unless there's something you haven't told me."

"No, we weren't," I admit.

"Drink your water." He sighs while I take a big gulp. "Listen, I know I give you shit a lot of the time, but I'm genuinely sorry that happened. You don't deserve that."

"Maybe I do."

"You don't."

"So, why does it keep happening to me? I wasn't enough for Blake. I'm not enough for Jake."

"You named two men. Two. Out of millions in this city alone," he points out. "I mean, sure, not every guy is gonna be dating material, but still. There's gotta be hundreds or thousands out there who would know how lucky they were to find a girl like you."

"Oh, please," I groan.

His couch is comfy. I lean against the cushions with a sigh.

"I mean, not me in particular," he adds. "We'd kill each other within a day or two. I'm surprised we haven't found a way to do that yet, honestly. God knows you take me to the point where I have to wonder if prison would be so bad after all."

"Shut up. Like you're any better with the damn screams and violins."

He covers his mouth with his hand, eyes wide. "Ah, man! Did that go off when you two were—"

"Yeah. Like, moments later. I swear, the timing couldn't have been better." I roll my head to the side, so I can glare at him. "Don't you dare."

All he can do is nod with his hand still over his mouth.

"I'm serious," I slur. "Don't."

He lifts his shoulders, nodding again. This time, the tiniest squeak comes out from between his fingers.

It's pointless. "I hate you so much."

He bursts out laughing and then leans away from me, so I can't reach when I take a swing at him.

"Don't laugh at me!"

He shakes his head, frantically waving his hands until they blur. Or maybe that's just me being drunk. "I'm not … laughing at you …It's just … oh hell …" He has to take a tissue for himself to wipe the tears from his eyes. "The timing. Oh my God, that must've been perfect." A fresh round of giggles comes after this.

The thing is, it was sort of perfect.

"At least I didn't have to scream," I admit with a tiny giggle. "It was like what was going on in my head happened out loud."

He falls back against the cushions, laughing again. "I probably couldn't do something that perfect again if I tried."

Now, I'm laughing too. "If … if it never happened, we'd probably still be lying there … not talking … the police would find us in a few days … once the stink got to be too much!"

It feels so good to laugh. Even better than crying.

Yes, this is a ridiculous situation. So silly, so pointless. And not anything that will kill me.

By the time we both wind down to nothing more than the occasional giggle, I can see things more clearly than before.

"Listen," Matt says once we can talk without losing it, "this is his loss. Big time. I'm sure he regrets it. And you did the right thing. He's got shit to work through before he can have another girl in his life. It's just a shame you were the one who had to help him see that."

"Yeah, it is a shame," I have to agree as I stroke Phoebe's head. She's still super confused over what all that noise was about, and she needs to be calmed, the sweet thing. "It's okay, honey. Everything's okay."

And it is, or it will be. I think.

"Look at it this way," Matt suggests with a smirk. "At least you got a book out of it."

"Shut up," I warn. "Too soon."

"There can't be much a nice, fat advance won't make up for." He shrugs.

I can't argue with that, so I don't bother.

Chapter Twenty-Two

*"I*F IT WASN'T *for you, I'd be lost. Always running from one place to the next without the first clue why I was running. Or why I was doing anything—because before you came along, there was no reason for my life. I pretended it was all for my patients, but I know now that isn't enough. I realize, I was missing the other half of myself. You."*

Maggie's a little breathless, a little swoony once she reaches the end of that passage. Why she felt the need to read it aloud is a mystery to me. I guess that means she loves it.

"I love it," Maggie gushes. "I absolutely love it. It's the perfect mix of sweet and heat. That whole scene in the motel room … whew! Tell me that was drawn from real life."

I roll my eyes, walking down the street while chatting with her on the phone. "Sorry to disappoint you."

"No kidding!"

"No kidding."

"Well, well, well! Look whose imagination suddenly decided to sprout wings and take flight!" She chortles. "Of course, I take full credit for this turn of events."

"Of course you do." I smile through my gritted teeth.

"Well? Who else is responsible? If it wasn't for me, you'd still be writing about florists and candy-shop owners."

"There's nothing wrong with florists or candy-shop owners."

"You know what I mean. Hell, you could write about a florist who takes it up the ass in the back room of her store, and I'd be fine with that."

Jeez, I sure hope nobody can hear her as I pass them on the sidewalk. But who am I kidding? Nobody pays attention to anybody else in the middle of Manhattan. They're all busy with their own phone calls and podcasts and audiobooks and music.

"I'll take that under consideration," I offer with a sigh.

"Ooh, and some sensory play with the flowers would be nice too ..."

"Okay, I'll make note of that. Thanks for the input."

"We're thinking of the title for the current book now," she informs me. "*Her Dirty Doctor* is the one at the top of the list. What do you think?"

"I think it doesn't matter whether I like the title or not. You're going to go with whatever sounds better to you. But wasn't there a podcast not long ago about a doctor, and it had the word *dirty* in it?"

"Hmm. I'll have to look into that. You know I don't pay attention to podcasts and the like."

No, she's too busy reading about shifters impregnating girls against their will and stuff like that. She makes it sound like podcasts are beneath her.

"Anyway, so long as you're happy and the book gets published, I'm okay with it." And I am.

It's getting easier to write the way she wants me to, the way the current market demands I do. I imagined it would be beneath me, but that's not true at all.

I needed to challenge myself and stretch my muscles, and I have.

Now, I need to come up with the next sucker—or rather, the next man to date. Just the thought of it makes me groan softly.

"Can I ask you something?" Maggie suddenly adds, just when I thought the conversation was over.

"Sure." I have a few more blocks to walk anyway, and without her to distract me, there's no telling where my thoughts might go.

"Are you happy? Writing this way, I mean. Does it fulfill you?"

What a question. I figured she'd ask if I could include more anal play in the next book. Maggie manages to surprise me, even after working with her for several years.

"I guess? I haven't thought about it," I admit.

"I've been too busy trying to keep my career afloat to worry about whether I'm fulfilled by my work."

This is a new direction for us. She's never taken the time to ask personal questions like this. I've always figured she looks at me as a word monkey who bangs against a keyboard all day until something worthwhile comes out.

"I don't want you to think I don't care," she explains. "I do. While I need books that will sell and you've done a great job so far, I don't want to think they've come at the expense of your self-respect and happiness with your work."

Is she serious? I almost want to ask that very question—and I would, if I didn't know it would insult her up and down. I sorta like this softer side my editor's been hiding from me all this time.

"Lois has been concerned too," she adds, which just about makes me drop the phone.

"I was afraid I didn't have an agent anymore after she left me high and dry." I snort.

It's been weeks since I've even heard from her—and that was nothing more than a congratulatory note after my first sexy book was picked up by the publisher.

"You do. Though you hardly need her at this point."

"You wouldn't be interested in cutting me loose from my agent, so you can offer whatever you want without a go-between telling me to ask for more money, would you?" I ask with a knowing grin.

Lois might be getting on in years, and she might have a bad habit of falling asleep in the middle of meetings, but she's a shrewd one when it comes to negotiating.

"Never!" Maggie gasps just a little louder than she should.

We leave it there and say our good-byes before I slide the phone into my pocket as I enter the dog park.

Instantly, two familiar huskies come running up to meet me.

"Hi, boys," I murmur, kissing their heads and loving on them. "How've you been? Have you been good boys? Not terrorizing any tiny dogs around here, are you?"

"You should have a dog."

I look up from where I'm crouched in front of the dogs. "You know, I've been thinking that lately myself. Goodness knows I'm home enough of the time. They wouldn't even have to miss me."

This is the reason I was glad for Maggie's call as I walked to the park. I knew I'd drive myself nuts if I was left to my own devices and worried about this little meeting all through my walk.

I've already done enough worrying ever since Jake texted me yesterday to ask if I had time to meet up.

Why? I still don't know. I don't have anything to be worried about. In the weeks since that disastrous night in my bed, I've made peace with how things went down. This was never supposed to be forever, no matter how nice it would've been if forever had been in the cards.

That, and working my fingers to the bone has been enough to get me through it.

Though now? Now, I'm in front of him. I can smell his cologne. I can see his ... everything. All of him. And darned if he doesn't still affect me physically, just the way he always has. I want to climb him and never come down.

I'm a grown-up. I can juggle knowing this isn't right with knowing I'll never stop being attracted to him. And not just because he's disgustingly gorgeous.

Because he's a decent man. A sweetheart. He deserves to be happy.

"How've you been?" he asks as the dogs trot off to have fun with their buddies.

"Good. Finished the book and slogged through the edits. My editor's happy with it, says they're already coming up with titles." I mime wiping sweat from my brow with the back of my hand. "So, that's a relief."

He nods, smiling just a little. But the smile doesn't reach his eyes, which look flat. "I didn't mean that—not just that anyway. Though I'm glad."

"I'd be happy to send you an advance copy, so you'll see how complimentary I was," I offer. "I didn't bad-mouth you or anything like that. In fact, your character ends up saving the heroine's life."

"How?"

I hold up a finger, wagging it back and forth. "You'll have to read it. No spoilers."

That gets a chuckle out of him anyway. "How are you though? How've you been … personally?"

Personally? There's a question I suspect he'd regret having asked if he had any idea.

"I've been working. Too busy to worry about anything else," I admit with a shrug.

He doesn't believe me. I can't blame him.

"What about you? How've you been?" *Since, ya know, you're the one who moaned your ex-girlfriend's name in my ear moments before entering me.*

I don't think the onus is on me to lead this conversation. Am I wrong? I don't think I'm wrong.

"I've been doing a lot of thinking," he begins, shoving his balled-up fists into his pockets and rocking back and forth from heel to toe. "Like you suggested. Like I needed to do."

"That's good." I have to bite the sides of my tongue to keep from blurting out the hundred or so questions racing around in my head, competing to see which one gets out first.

"And there's definitely no chance of anything happening with Erin and me ever again. I want to make sure you know that," he adds, looking from the dogs to me. "That was never an option. Never on the table. I wasn't lying when I told you how things fell apart for us. We'll never be on the same page again."

"I'm glad for you. I mean that. You're doing so well as you are, the way you've changed your life. I'd hate to see you turn into some uptight, stressed-out machine."

"You and me both." He scuffs the toe of his shoe against the ground, looking down at it. "Still, I have things to get through. I made myself stop thinking about her when she left, told myself it was over. The end. Maybe that wasn't the smart way to go."

"We do what we can."

"I guess so. All I know is, I don't want to hurt you. I need you to know that."

"I do."

When he holds out his arms, there's nothing for me to do but go to him. I need one more of his big hugs even if something inside twists and tightens when his arms close around me.

Darn it. This could've been good.

"I don't want you to have to be around me while I'm trying to get over somebody I know I have no future with," he murmurs against the top of my head. "That's not fair to you."

"You're right," I have to admit. "No hard feelings. And no hard feelings about me killing you at the end of my book."

"What?" he gasps, holding me at arm's length. "Are you kidding?"

"Yes!" I laugh. "Rule number one: happily ever after. I can't kill the hero. *Jeez.*"

Happily ever after. Is there such a thing? I write about it all the time, don't I?

But do I believe it actually exists?

Something Matt told me that night rings out in my memory. I just haven't found the right one yet. *The happily ever after one.*

That doesn't mean he's not out there.

"I'd better get these guys home," he says before calling them over and clipping their leashes to their collars. He looks and sounds relieved, which I can certainly relate to. Like he was dreading this the way I was.

"Maybe I'll run into you in the ER sometime?" I suggest with a grin when he turns my way one last time.

I wish I could freeze him like this, right here, with the dogs by his side and sunshine bringing out the gold streaks in his hair and eyes. Smiling.

He shakes his head. "Is it wrong to say I hope not?"

"No. I guess it's pretty nice actually. Though odds are, I'll probably be back sometime. I can't make any promises."

"I'll keep an eye out for you." He winks and then, "Oh. One more thing."

"What?"

"Learn to have a little fun. Life's about more than working in your apartment. Make it a point to get out sometimes, just to live. Okay?"

He's right. If there's anything I've learned from

him besides the proper way to perform the Heimlich maneuver, it's the importance of stepping away from work and turning my attention to my actual life. Funny, but being with Blake should've taught me that.

Jake drove the point home and showed me it's possible to have a life. There I was, thinking I was so much better at striking a balance than Blake was.

"I will," I vow before waving one last time and walking away.

Chapter Twenty-Three

I MUST'VE BEEN out of my mind for a minute when I figured spending more time with my grandmother would be the first step toward creating an actual life, the way Jake inspired me to do.

It's always easier to handle her in my mind than it is in person. Especially when she's staring at me like I grew a second head—and all because I made the fatal mistake of suggesting she read my work.

"I thought you should read it." I nudge the advance copy of my latest book across the dining room table, toward Grandmother. "Now that your friends have seen me in the last couple of months, they might be likelier to pick this up if they run past it, and you should know the sort of stuff that's in there, just in case."

She eyes the book like I just dropped a cockroach on the table. "Is it … violent? I thought you wrote romance and love."

"I do. There isn't any violence."

She looks from the book to me, eyes wide with confusion. "Why do I need to read it then?"

"Are you seriously doing this to me?" I whisper

while my cheeks flame up.

We're both grown women, and goodness knows she doesn't normally have a problem with talking about sex and men and all that stuff.

Why is she playing dumb with me now?

"I don't understand. Help me under—"

"Sex, Grandmother. There's lots of sex. Detailed sex."

She doesn't flinch or even blink. "And?"

"And … you might want to be aware of that." I lean in a little, studying her. *Is she for real?* If not, she has an awfully good poker face. "You mean, it doesn't matter whether there's sex in there or not?"

"No."

"It doesn't embarrass you?"

"No! What's so embarrassing about sex?" She throws a hand into the air, scoffing. "Please. It's the one thing we all have in common, darling. The thing that got us here—almost all of us anyway, excluding scientific measures. You know what I mean."

"It doesn't make you uneasy? Knowing I wrote it?"

"Heavens, no. You always manage to underestimate me, Kathryn. You should know by now that I'm no prude." She takes a sip of her martini. "I didn't have a problem with that last book you wrote. By the way, I had no idea you released books so frequently now. You aren't working too hard, are you?"

"Whoa. Wait a sec." *My mind is being blown as we speak.* "You read the last book? You've read my books?"

Her glass clinks against the table. Rings glitter as she folds her hands. "Were you under the misconception that I would avoid reading my granddaughter's books for any reason? Did you believe anything in the world could've kept me from reading your work?"

Just when I thought there was no blowing my mind any further. "You never want to talk about it."

"Oh, please. Talking about work? How gauche." There's a twinkle in her eye and just the tiniest smile tugging at her scarlet lips. "I must say, I'm sorry you took my reticence as a sign of my not caring. Nothing could be further from the truth."

"I underestimated you."

"It appears you did." She sniffs, but her eyes are still twinkling. "For what it's worth, you are an excellent writer. No matter the level of … spice."

"You think so?"

"I think so, as do thousands or even millions of readers, darling. At such a young age, you are a huge success. I must say, I envy you."

"Me? Why would you envy me?" What an afternoon this has been for surprises.

"You know what it is you want to do with your life. You have a talent and the means by which to use that talent. Do you know how many people live their entire lives without any of those things? Far too many."

Does that mean she's one of those people?

"Did you do what you wanted?" I ask, and it occurs to me that we've never had a conversation like this. So open and honest with so many of the carefully constructed walls between us crumbling.

They're thin, those walls, and invisible for the most part. But they're there. I think it must come from her breeding, not to mention the time she came from.

She gives me a blithe shrug. "I did what I did. I married who I was supposed to marry. Don't get me wrong; I don't regret it for a minute. I would rather have had twelve years with your grandfather than a lifetime with any man. Once he was gone, I had your mother to fill my time. My life. I can't say I would change much that was within my power to change."

She didn't exactly answer my question, did she?

Yes, she did. Not flat out, not in so many words, but I understand. She has regrets. Too many people do.

I guess it's up to me to make sure I have fewer than she does by the time I'm her age.

"So, I take it, you've broken things off with your doctor friend." She picks up her knife and fork to flake off a piece of salmon, though she never stops looking at me.

"Boy, you won't even give me a chance to recover before you go in for another punch," I groan. "Yes. It was a mutual decision."

"You didn't lock him down."

"I did not."

"I warned you that you'd better lock him down."

"I couldn't help what happened. He wasn't ready to be with me. Or anybody." No matter how easygoing and progressive she is when it comes to sex, there are certain things I have no desire to discuss with her.

She doesn't need to hear about his little faux pas.

"I'm sorry to hear that," she sighs, shaking her head. "What a waste. Though there's no telling how he'll feel in six months, darling. I wouldn't go erasing his phone number from your cell, in other words."

"I know what you mean. But I don't want to look desperate. Besides, if I'm going to write about another sort of man, I have to try to date that sort of man. I can't tie myself down to any one person right now."

"I don't know how I feel about that."

"I'm being perfectly safe and responsible," I make sure to say even though talking to her about things like this makes my skin crawl.

"I'm not talking about that. I'm talking about you wasting the prime of your life, dating men simply for the sake of writing about them. Who do you have to date next time? A circus performer? Perhaps someone who eats fire? Or an exterminator? Not exactly the sort of person I want to see you settle down with."

"Nobody ever said anything about settling down."

"One day, you'll have to."

"Says who?"

"Says your grandmother, young lady. Do you expect me to leave this life someday without knowing you're going to be taken care of?"

"I don't need to be taken care of."

"I can't say I agree." She goes in for more salmon. "Not hungry?"

"I'm sorry." I have to put down my silverware. "I'm not. Talking about Jake has me a little sad. That's all."

She puts her silverware down too. "My dear, I didn't think. I apologize. He meant a good deal to you."

"He shouldn't have, but he did. This is the second time I've done this to myself in less than a few months—caring too much for someone when I know I shouldn't. I can't help it."

"You're a loving person," she murmurs. "It's in your nature. You remind me so much of your mother sometimes. She loved with her entire heart freely. I was never able to love that way, so exuberantly."

I have to smile at the memory. "She was a big hugger. She'd squeeze until I was sure she was breaking my ribs. But I miss those hugs so much."

"It's a beautiful thing, being able to love that way. But"—she lowers her brow—"not at the expense of one's heart. You must know where to draw a line between being open to wonderful things and protecting yourself."

"I'm learning that. The hard way."

"Sadly, that's the only way of learning such lessons. Wouldn't it be lovely if one could simply know everything without going through pain? But how boring life would be."

Once again, I want to be her when I grow up.

"I'm sorry though." I wince. "I know you said I was out of the will if I didn't lock Jake down."

"This is true. I did say that."

"I guess you can give everything away rather than leaving it to me."

Another smile makes her lips twitch. "I suppose I can overlook my threat—this time. Though I can't make any promises for the future."

"That's all right." I shrug, picking up my silverware now that my appetite seems to be surging back. "I don't plan on needing any of the family money. I'll build my own empire."

"I have no doubt that you will do just that." She smiles before adding, "But your inheritance is still there, just in case."

Honestly, I expected that.

ABOUT THE AUTHOR

Jillian Dodd is a USA Today bestselling mother-daughter duo made up of Jill and Kenzie—two writers, one pen name, and a shared love for fun, binge-worthy YA romance.

With over fifty books and millions of happy readers, their stories range from small-town love in *That Boy* to glamorous adventures and swoony YA boarding school dramas in *The Keatyn Chronicles, London Prep, Spy Girl,* and beyond.

Jill lives in sunny Florida with her husband, while Kenzie lives in Scotland with her husband and family. When they're not writing across time zones, you'll find them planning their next adventure or dreaming up lovable stories readers can't put down.

Check out our books and swag at www.jilliandodd.net

www.ingramcontent.com/pod-product-compliance
Lightning Source LLC
LaVergne TN
LVHW091135080826
845145LV00008B/2165